I0690714

VOLUME TWO

AIRSHIP 27 PRODUCTIONS

Domino Lady-Volume Two
The Domino Lady's Justice © 2016 Gene Moyers
The Domino Lady's Triple Threat © 2016 Brad Mengel
The Murder Games © 2016 Robert M. Ricci
The Domino Lady & the Spy Squad © 2016 Kevin Findley

Published by Airship 27 Productions
www.airship27.com
www.airship27hangar.com

Cover illustration © 2016 Ted Hammond
Interior illustrations © 2016 James Lyle

Editor: Ron Fortier
Associate Editor: Jaime Ramos
Marketing and Promotions Manager: Michael Vance
Production and design: Rob Davis.

ISBN-10: 1-946183-01-6
ISBN-13: 978-1-946183-01-9

Printed in the United States of America

10 9 8 7 6 5 4 3 2 1

Domino Lady
Volume Two
Table of Contents

THE DOMINO LADY'S JUSTICE............................5

Gene Moyers

When one of Ellen Patrick's dearest friends commits suicide, she suspects foul play and it's up to the Domino Lady to uncover the truth of statewide political corruption.

THE DOMINO LADY'S TRIPLE THREAT.............43

Brad Mengel

When an old family friend is kidnapped by a group of American Nazis Bundists, it is up to the Domino Lady to find and rescue him.

THE MURDER GAMES...78

Robert M. Ricci

In her attempt to promote the city of Los Angeles for the Olympics, Ellen Patrick runs afoul of German spies.

THE DOMINO LADY & THE SPY SQUAD.........124

Kevin Findley

Private Eye Roger McKane seeks the Domino Lady's aid in bringing down a gang of corrupt policemen whose primary trade is the blackmailing of city government officials.

THE DOMINO LADY'S JUSTICE

Gene Moyers

*I*t was a beautiful day for driving. Ellen Patrick had the top down on her roadster and reveled in the sun on her face. The wind streaming across the open car attempted to whip her lush blonde hair from under the scarf she had covered it with. She smiled as she steered the powerful automobile north on Highway 99. It was a long drive from the Los Angeles basin but she had made good time and she was nearing Sacramento. She thought hopefully about finally arriving in the state's capital and checking into her hotel room. It would be good to stretch, and there was just enough time to take a leisurely bath before she met Steve for dinner.

Steve; it was certainly pleasurable thinking about Steve Pearce. She had met him years ago at Berkeley. They hadn't dated then. He had actually been dating her roommate at the time. He was two years ahead of her and when he had graduated they had lost touch. She remembered him as a handsome young pre-law student who had been a big man on campus. Ellen had met him again a few weeks ago at a Hollywood party. If anything he had gotten better looking and he was successful to boot. It turned out he was a lawyer working in the Attorney General's office out of Sacramento. They had kept in touch by letter and phone and been on a few dates together. Ellen liked him. He was intelligent and funny and not stuffy as many lawyers were. When he invited Ellen to a ball to be held at the executive mansion she had jumped at the chance. She had bought a new dress especially for the occasion and hoped that Steve would like it.

Soon Ellen reached the outskirts of Sacramento and navigated her way through the city streets to the *Meridian* hotel. The hotel had her reservation ready and in a few minutes she was inspecting her suite. It had been a long trip and she left her unpacking for later and began filling the tub for a bath. Soon she was relaxing in luxuriously scented warm bath water. She decided that the only thing she lacked was a glass of champagne. Unfortunately the *Meridian* was far too respectable to be serving bootleg alcohol.

Ellen dozed in the warm water. She woke with a jerk and glanced at the clock. She had promised to call Steve. She stood up, the water sluicing off her svelte body and long legs. She stepped out of the tub and wrapped a towel around her before heading for the living room. She was just reaching for the phone when it jangled insistently. Startled, she jerked her hand back for an instant before picking up the receiver, "Hello?"

A calm male voice replied, "Miss Patrick? This is Mark at the front desk, I'm sorry to say there is a message here for you. We should have given it to you when you checked in. It was delivered earlier today but we had misplaced it. I'm terribly sorry if this has inconvenienced you. We can send it up right away."

Ellen replied with a smile, "Don't worry about it Mark and please do send it up." Ellen then went to find a robe. A few minutes later there was a knock on the suite's door. When she opened it there was a young, uniformed bell boy waiting with an envelope in his hand. He proffered the note while trying not to stare at Ellen's alluring figure; barely concealed beneath her thin silk robe. Ellen pressed a dime into his hand before shutting the door on his still awestruck face. Ellen glanced at the envelope; it was addressed to her at the *Meridian* hotel. The handwriting was Steve's. She excitedly tore the open the envelope and opened the single sheet of note paper. It read:

Dear Ellen,

I am writing this even as you are on your way. I tried to reach you early this morning to stop you from coming but you had already left. I'm terribly sorry, but we will not be able to attend the ball tomorrow. In fact, I cannot see you at all this weekend. It is too dangerous. I know this is surprising to you but things have suddenly changed.

Lately, I have been working closely with the Attorney General on special projects that he has assigned me. I did this gladly thinking that it would help me along in my career. Recently I became suspicious of some of the things the Attorney General was involved in and the things he had me working on. I began documenting these things and covertly researching the AG's activities. I now strongly believe he is somehow involved in corruption involving a wealthy and powerful individual. Others may be involved as well. I have collected all the documentation into one file that I intend to turn over to the press as I can trust no one here in the office or anywhere in the state government. The information in this file is extremely incriminating not only for the AG's office but for others highly placed in state government. Unfortunately I now believe that I am under suspicion and being watched. I have hidden the key to the file's location and must go into hiding.

This is why I cannot see you this weekend. It is too dangerous for you. Go home, say nothing and pretend you never met me. Perhaps when the dust settles we may be able to start again. I am sorry to bring these troubles on you. I would do things differently if I had the chance.

"O, I am fortune's fool!"

Take care,

Steve

As Ellen read the letter the smile fell of her face and she went pale. When finished, she crumpled the letter in her hand and rushed for the telephone. Furiously she dialed Steve's home number. The phone rang and kept ringing. As she was about to hang up, the receiver was picked up and a man's voice spoke carefully, "Hello?"

It was not Steve's voice. Ellen questioned, "Who is this?"

There was a hesitation and then, "This is the police. Who is this?"

Ellen slammed down the receiver and ran for the bedroom. In minutes she had thrown on a dress and shoes, grabbed her car keys and ran from the suite, the door slamming shut behind her. She ran for the elevator and begged the operator to take her to the lobby quickly. Once down she hurried across the lobby and out the front door of the hotel. She waited impatiently while her car was brought around and threw herself behind the wheel. She was only passingly familiar with Sacramento streets but she still managed to reach Steve's apartment building in less that fifteen minutes.

She skidded the roadster to a stop across the street from Steve's four story apartment building. Ominously, there were two police cruisers parked in front of it and a police officer stood at the front door. She walked briskly across the street and up the steps. She pasted a smile on her face and tried to breeze past the officer but he put out a hand to stop her, "Do you live here miss?"

Ellen replied casually, "I'm visiting someone who lives here. Is there a problem officer?"

"The Lieutenant says no one goes in or out. You'll have to wait here." He opened the door entered the hallway and called something up the stairwell. He then returned to Ellen, "The Lieutenant will be down in a minute." Ellen tried to look casual but interested while inside her heart was sinking. Police here could not be good. What had happened?

Minute later a middle-aged man wearing a somewhat rumpled suit appeared in the doorway. He motioned to Ellen to enter the building. Once in the hall he removed an unlit cigar from his mouth and spoke, "Who are you?"

Ellen didn't hesitate, "My name is April Dale."

The detective looked her over carefully, "Yeah? Who are you looking for?"

"I'm here to see Steve Pearce. He's a friend."

The plain clothes man kept his face neutral, "Are you close to Pearce?"

Ellen attempted to hold her emotions in as she feared the worst, "We're friends and we have a date tonight."

The cop looked emotionless as he broke the news she had feared, "I'm sorry miss but I have bad news for you. Mr. Pearce was found dead in his apartment a short while ago."

Ellen had prepared herself but hearing the words still threw her heart into her throat. She swallowed and tried to hold back tears. She took a deep breath and asked, "What happened?" The detective was watching her closely as he pulled a notebook out of one coat pocket. He opened it and asked, "What did you say your name was?"

Ellen frowned, "April Dale, and I asked what happened to Steve?" The detective wrote in his notebook and said without looking up, "It looks like Mr. Pearce took his own life, I'm afraid." He looked up in time to see Ellen's pale face, her lips pressed tightly together. He started to say something, hesitated and then spoke more softly, "I'm sorry about your friend. Can you tell me when you spoke with him last?"

In a monotone Ellen answered, "Yesterday, he was looking forward to my visit."

"He didn't sound sad or upset?"

"No, of course not. Steve was happy. He had no reason to do something like this. Are you sure it wasn't some kind of accident or foul play?" Ellen was fast regaining her composure and her mind was racing ahead. She knew that Steve hadn't committed suicide. The letter told her that. She needed to see him and his apartment.

The detective shook his head, "We're sure it wasn't an accident or foul play. He had a pen and paper on his desk as if he was ready to write a letter...or a suicide note. Then he must have changed his mind. His pistol was still in his hand. A new box of ammunition had just been opened." That was the last straw. Ellen looked the cop straight in the eye and gritted out, "Steve didn't have any reason to kill himself. He was a successful attorney working for the Attorney General's office. What's more he didn't even own a gun. He told me that he didn't need one since he was a lawyer. He believed in the law."

The jaded cop tried hard not to look skeptical, "Look Miss uh, Dale, this must be hard for you. Is there someone you can call, a friend perhaps?" Ellen tried to get the detective to see reason, "Look why would he invite me here from out of town just to kill himself. We were going to a ball at the governor's mansion tomorrow."

The detective kept his face neutral, "Look Miss, I know something like this is hard to accept but the evidence is overwhelming." Ellen realized she wasn't going to get much help from this detective. He had already made up his mind. It was obvious he wanted a quick solution so he could get home for dinner. Her emotions boiled inside but she tried to remain calm. She took a breath and spoke, "I'm sorry detective uh..."

"Morgan, ma'am. Lieutenant Morgan."

"Lieutenant Morgan, if you're right I'm sure everything will come out after your investigation. The autopsy and your search of his apartment will bring everything to light." The detective took his cigar out of his mouth and inspected it. He looked slightly embarrassed. Ellen realized that there would probably be no investigation. A chill ran down her back. Was this just police laziness or was there something more sinister behind this white wash? She decided that she would learn nothing more here.

Detective Morgan tried to change the subject. He held up his notebook and asked, "Do you have any way to contact his next of kin?"

Ellen glanced at her watch, "Of course, you're right. There are people who need to be notified. I'm certain his family will want to come down to make arrangements."

Detective Morgan seemed a relieved, "Of course Miss. The apartment is a crime scene but we should release it in a couple of days. The family should call the coroner's office to make arrangements for the uh...for Mr. Pearce."

Ellen wasn't listening. She had no intentions of calling anyone or helping with any arrangements. Her mind was racing ahead with plans. She gave Morgan a weak smile and thanked him before turning away and walking briskly across the street to her roadster. As she was getting inside

Morgan suddenly remembered his job and yelled out, "Uh miss Dale, How do we get in touch with you?" Ellen smiled at him as she threw the powerful car into gear and accelerated down the street.

As she cruised back to her hotel Ellen shuffled through the possibilities in her mind. Steve had been right. He had been in danger. Ellen was certain there had been no suicide or accident. Whatever Steve had found out was important enough to get him murdered. His note was proof of that. He had been right in warning Ellen off too. If only he had followed his own advice and gotten away sooner he might still be alive. Her breath caught in her throat as she thought of him but a moment later she was all business again. Steve had said in his note that he had evidence; a file. But what had happened to it. Had his murderers forced Steve to give it to them before he was killed? She needed more facts. She needed to see his apartment and as horrible as it would be she had to See Steve's body or talk to the coroner who would examine it.

As Ellen neared her hotel she knew what she had to do. She found a parking spot against the curb down the street from the *Meridian*. It would give her easy access later on. She walked back to her hotel, crossed the luxurious lobby and had the elevator operator take her to her floor. It was nearing sunset and she had not eaten since lunch in Bakersfield but Ellen was not hungry. She sat in a chair near a window and watched the room darken as the sun set. She lit a cigarette and waited wishing she had a drink.

Hours later a beautiful blonde woman in a long white dress crossed the lobby of the *Meridian* hotel. Her height was accented by her black high heels. The dress and fur stole across her shoulders spoke of wealth. Her carriage and beauty spoke of class. She received more than one admiring glance from male passersby.

Once on the sidewalk the doorman summoned a taxi with a wave of his hand. He held the door for her as she entered it. Inside she told the driver to take her south. He nodded and dropped the flag. The taxi cruised away and Ellen tried to look casual although she was actually keyed up inside. Several blocks later she told the driver she had forgotten something and wanted to return to the hotel. He obligingly turned the cab around. Ellen had him drop her at the corner. He was slightly surprised but said nothing as she paid him and sent him on his way. When he was out of sight she crossed the street to her car.

She fired up the roadster and guided the big car slowly across town. It was nearly ten o'clock. The police should have left Steve's apartment by now. If so she hoped that they hadn't left any guards on duty. She soon reached Steve's street and drove past his building at a normal pace looking things over. The police cars were gone. The apartment building seemed normal with lights on in various apartments. She nodded and cruised to the corner pulling over and parking near the mouth of an alley that ran behind Steve's street. From the shadowy interior of the car Ellen looked carefully around but saw no one.

Certain she was unwatched; Ellen reached into her purse and placed several items on the seat next to her. She lifted the hem of her long white dress and slipped a slim automatic pistol into a special holster attached to the inside of one shapely thigh. Into a stretch holder on the other leg she slid a glass syringe capped with cork. She then picked up the last item, a black domino mask and arranged it over her face. In the shadows of the car Ellen Patrick had vanished, replaced by the exotic figure of the Domino Lady.

She tossed the stole into the back seat and replaced it with a long black cloak. Quickly she was out of the car and making her way carefully down the darkened alley. In the alley the only light came from shaded windows but it was enough for the Domino Lady to avoid obstacles and move nearly silently. In less than a minute she reached the back of the building that she was sure was where Steve's apartment was. There was a fire escape running up the back of the building but the ladder was above her head. Frustrated she considered picking the back door lock for a moment and then spied a cylindrical shadow against a wall. It was a metal garbage can that she quickly moved under the fire escape. Despite her long dress and heels Domino Lady quickly climbed up, balanced for a moment and grabbed the ladder. Moments later she was on the second floor landing.

The apartment in front of her was dark although she could hear muffled voices and even music coming from other apartments nearby. She nodded and quietly climbed the metal stairs to the third floor metal landing. There were two windows in front of her, both dark. If she remembered correctly the right one led to Steve's bedroom the left one opened into the apartment next door. The right hand window was locked. Domino Lady reached into a small pocket hidden in her cloak and withdrew a metal lock pick. She inserted it vertically between the upper and lower window sashes and moved it back and forth until she found the latch. It took but a moment's manipulation to push it back and clear of the sash. She replaced her lock pick and silently lifted the sash.

She lifted one leg across the sill and in a moment was standing in the darkened bedroom. She paused to listen but the apartment was both dark and silent. Nodding she turned and drew the drapes across the window then crossed the room to switch on the overhead light. It was Steve's bedroom and she had a momentary pang of sadness but shook it off. His bedroom was as good a place as any to start searching. She made a quick but thorough search. She was looking for a file of documents as Steve had described it. It must be fairly large and bulky, not something that could be hidden in a rolled up sock. His dresser drawers held only clothes. There was nothing under the bed or between the mattresses. The closet held Steve's shoes and a good sized collection of suits but not much else; some luggage and his tennis racket and some balls. Tennis; that was Steve's kind of sport. They had talked of athletics and hobbies and that was when Steve had stated that he knew nothing of guns.

Finished with the bedroom Domino Lady turned off the light and made her way down the hall. She turned on the light and glanced into the living room but quickly decided that wasn't the place for hiding bulky, valuable items and turned off the light. She decided to save the kitchen for last and instead turned to the second bedroom that Steve had turned into an office.

Entering she flipped on the light and took a good look around. Steve had had wood workers build a floor to ceiling book case along one wall. Opposite this was his desk. A file cabinet stood in one corner, a comfortable chair and reading light in another. Taking a deep breath she stepped to the desk. As she suspected there was a large dark stain on the desk blotter and floor underneath. The desk chair had been pushed back. Looking closely the Domino Lady could see fine black powder on the desk and chair. So at least the police had been professional enough to dust for finger prints. Carefully she slid open the desk's large center drawer and began her search. The first thing she found was an engraved white envelope. Opening it she found an engraved invitation. It was addressed to Steve and read: *The honorable Clement C. Young desires the presence of Steven Pearce Esq. and guest at the Governor's Ball to be held...*It was their invitation to the ball. Controlling her emotions Domino Lady tucked the invitation away and continued searching. There were lots of papers and documents in the desk but almost all of them were personal; an appointment calendar, letters and checkbooks but little else of importance.

She then turned to the file cabinet. This was more interesting as it contained nothing but work briefs and case files. The Domino Lady quickly scanned through the numerous files looking for interesting names and titles. Twenty minutes of searching turned up nothing.

The Domino Lady quickly scanned through the numerous files...

Although she found nothing concrete it was apparent that files were missing. There were card markers in between files holding the place of something removed and there several topics that had glaring gaps in dates. The Domino Lady frowned behind her mask. The question was, which files had Steve removed himself and were any taken by someone else? If Steve had removed critical files where would he have hidden them?

As she thought through this puzzle she found she was staring at Steve's bookshelves. She took a step closer. As expected there were several sets of matching law books. Then there were Steve's personal books: novels, a few pulp magazines, some classics including Shakespeare, Dickens and Poe and surprisingly several books on poetry. Perhaps that was where the quote in his note had come from. It had seemed vaguely familiar to her. There was also a large selection of history books and biographies of historical figures. The Domino Lady thought this interesting until she remembered that Steve had taken his undergraduate degree in history before attending law school. There was no room to hide a large file of information in any of the books but perhaps Steve had left a clue there.

The Domino Lady took a step toward the wall of books and froze. She had heard muffled voices nearby. She glided to the room's door flicking off the light switch as she reached it. In the darkness she could clearly hear a key rasping against a lock. She slid through the darkness toward the rear bedroom and reached it just as the hall door opened. A shaft of light stabbed into the darkened apartment from the open door. Domino Lady pressed herself against the door frame as she pulled her automatic from its hidden holster. She heard a voice whisper, "Close the door!" The hall door closed quietly again leaving the apartment in darkness.

In the living room flashlights clicked on. Whoever it was, it was not the police. They would not be whispering or be afraid of turning on lights. Deciding against a confrontation the Domino Lady slipped silently around the bed toward the window. Raising the sash with one hand she could see the wavering beams of flashlights moving down the hallway. She was just reaching one long leg over the sill of the window when a flashlight beam swept into the room catching her full in its beam. There was a shout from an unseen voice that was cut short by the Domino Lady's shot. Off balance she snapped off a quick shot aiming over the intruder's head. The .25 caliber slug dug into the wall above the door frame. There was a curse and the light went out.

Her gun in one hand the Domino Lady threw herself through the window onto the metal fire escape landing. She was halfway down the stairs to the second floor when she turned, took careful aim and fired a shot high through the upper sash of Steve's window. The trajectory would take it safely into the room's ceiling and hopefully discourage quick pursuit. She jumped the rest of the way to the second floor landing and from there was onto the ladder in two quick steps. She climbed down as far as she could and dropped into the darkened alley.

Holding the hem of her dress up with one hand she ran down the alley, her legs taking long strides toward the light at end of the block. She heard a distant curse followed by a shot that ricocheted off brick somewhere above her head and ran faster. Exiting onto the side street the Domino Lady hopped quickly into the roadster and pressed the starter. The engine roared to life. She shoved it into gear and sped away with a screech of rubber. She drove quickly for several blocks and then turned sharply right. At the next corner she took a left. She continued driving quickly and turning at random until she was sure there was no pursuit. When she felt safe she pulled over on a shadowy side street. There she removed her mask and moved her gun and hypodermic to her purse. She also exchanged her black cloak for her stole. Twenty minutes later she pulled up in front of the *Meridian* and gave her car over to the valet. She went straight to her suite. Later in bed it was a long time before Ellen closed her eyes. There was much to think about and plans to be made.

Over a leisurely breakfast Ellen considered the situation. Those two men at Steve's apartment could not have been police. Were they his killers? They were undoubtedly looking for the information Steve had hidden. Ellen considered this. If they had killed Steve why hadn't they searched for the files earlier? She frowned; of course! The suicide story wouldn't have held up if the apartment was torn apart by a search. The good news was that if they were still searching, the mysterious file must still be out there somewhere; but where?

Something was bothering Ellen; it was that quote in Steve's letter. It kept running through her mind, she knew it from somewhere. Then it struck her just how to find out what it was. But first she had a phone call to make. She picked up the receiver and asked the hotel operator to connect her with police headquarters. Once connected, she asked for Lieutenant Morgan. There was a wait and she was somewhat surprised to finally have him on the line. Since it was Saturday she wasn't sure he would be working?

"Lieutenant Morgan? This is April Dale. We met yesterday. I'm calling to find out if you've learned any more about the death of my friend, Steve Pearce."

"Oh...Miss Dale, I'm glad you called. We didn't get your contact information yesterday. We need it for our records."

Ellen hesitated. The same instinct that had made her give a phony name the day before was calling to her. She apologized for leaving so quickly and reeled off a totally fictitious address in Santa Barbara. She gave him a moment to write it down and then repeated her question, "Now Detective have you learned anything else?"

"Well, yes Miss Dale, we have. We have confirmation that the gun found in Mr. Pearce's hand was in fact registered in his name. We also have the coroner's finding that his death was a suicide. Since we found no finger prints or other signs of anyone else in his apartment we are concluding that his death was in fact a suicide. I'm just signing off on the report now." He paused before adding, "I'm sorry if that's not what you wanted to hear Miss, but that's what the evidence shows."

Ellen was taken aback for a moment then replied sarcastically, "That's a lot of conclusions this early in the morning isn't it? You found about this gun registration in less than 24 hours? And on a weekend to boot, that is impressive work. And an overnight autopsy. It's apparent that the Sacramento police department has moved heaven and earth on this case." Ellen paused and added, "And for just a routine suicide. Heaven knows what kind of effort you might put into a real murder case."

Detective Morgan's voice came back heatedly, "Just what are you implying Miss Dale?"

"I'm not implying anything. I'm just saying it seems like you've put together a lot of information and conclusions in a very short time. It seems to me that someone seems to want a very quick resolution of this case. Or am I just imagining it?"

There was another short but definite pause before the detective replied in a cold, calm voice, "Miss Dale I know you must be upset at the death of your friend but there's no need to become hysterical and start making rash accusations. That is only going to reflect badly on you." Ellen frowned, she did not like the tone of his voice. He continued, "People might begin to wonder about your state of mind." These words gave Ellen a chill. She spoke carefully, "I can see there's no more to be learned here. I'm returning immediately to Santa Barbara. Thank you Lieutenant." She then broke the connection.

Ellen stared thoughtfully at the telephone. Perhaps those men last night had been police after all. Someone had certainly put in "the fix." They wanted Steve's death to be swept under the rug as a suicide and be quickly forgotten. She suddenly badly wanted to be anywhere but here in the city, unfortunately there was still work to be done. She was now very glad that she had given the police a phony name and address. Anyone who went looking for her would not be looking for Ellen Patrick. She turned for the bedroom to get dressed.

An hour later Ellen pulled up in front of the main branch of the public library. She parked and hurried up the steps. Once inside she quickly located the information desk. As she approached, a middle aged lady in glasses who looked as if she had studied all her life to be the perfect image of a librarian smiled at her and spoke quietly, "Good day, may I help you?"

Ellen returned her smile and said, "I'm trying to run down a literary quote. I believe it comes from Shakespeare but I'm not sure."

"Can you tell me the quote?"

"Certainly. It goes, 'O, I am fortune's fool!' Do you know it?"

The lady smiled, "Yes, that's from Shakespeare alright. From *Romeo and Juliet* I believe. But let's check to be sure." She bent down and lifted a heavy looking leather bound reference book labeled *Bartlett's Quotations* onto the desk. She flipped through pages for nearly a minute and finally ran her finger down the page, "Yes, it's here. Romeo Act III, scene I, line 136." She closed the book and smiled at Ellen, "I hope that helps Miss."

Ellen smiled and nodded, "Thank you that helps immensely." Ellen inquired where she could find Shakespeare and was given directions. It did not take long to find a copy of *Romeo and Juliet*. She located the quote and read over that section of the play. The quote was by Romeo just after his friend Mercutio had been killed and he had slain Tybalt. She closed the book thoughtfully. Steve could have repeated it because he saw Romeo's guilt as a reflection of his own guilt and victimization. Perhaps he was calling out in anguish; Perhaps. As she turned and left the library Ellen was thinking of the Shakespeare book she had seen on Steve's bookshelf. By the time she reached her car she decided she needed to return to his apartment. She drove across town and cruised past the apartment building once more. Everything seemed quiet. No police cars, no uproar. The building looked as if nothing unusual had happened there in the last twenty four hours. Now was not the time to look around Ellen though. Later tonight she would be back. She turned the car for her hotel. Right now she had a ball to get ready for.

At just past eight o'clock that evening Ellen turned her car over to a va-let in front of the executive mansion and walked up the steps to entryway. Inside she was politely confronted by a formally dressed staff member. He smiled and said, "Good evening," and held out his hand. Ellen smiled back and handed him the engraved invitation. He glanced at it as he ran his fin-gernail across the raised letters and returned it to her with a smile, "Have a pleasant evening." Ellen thanked him and walked past him toward the noise of many voices. Either he had not even read the name on it or he had not been told to look out for anyone carrying Steve's invitation. Either way it worked out just the way Ellen had hoped. She checked her stole at the cloak room and entered the main ball room.

The large room was half filled with formally dressed men and women. A stringed quartet played in one corner. Passing waiters carried trays of hors-d'oeuvres and glasses of sparkling liquid among the guests. Elle re-lived a passing waiter of one of these glasses and sipped as she mingled with the crowd. She was only mildly surprised to find that it was sparkling cider. She had halfway expected the glass to contain champagne. Even in these days of Prohibition alcohol could be found everywhere. As she mingled she mentally shook her head, Prohibition just created corruption; as if there weren't enough of that everywhere you looked.

Ellen circulated. She was looking for people who might have worked with Steve and she spoke to as many people as she could without drawing attention to herself. It was easy to find young men who wanted to talk to her. Her royal blue dress was low cut to accent her ample bosom. It also set off her long blonde hair and her creamy complexion perfectly. She was asked to dance repeatedly and turned no one down. During these mostly pleasant forays she learned a lot. She asked someone point out the Attorney General. She also met three different people who knew Steve slightly but no one who worked with him or new him personally. During an interval between dances the Governor made his entrance to applause which Ellen cheerfully joined in.

She finally shook off her male admirers by excusing herself to go pow-der her nose. She did this when she saw the Attorney General heading in the direction of the restrooms. She was hoping for a private word. As she turned down the corridor leading to the restrooms she saw the Attorney General accosted by a tall, heavy set man. They exchanged words and went around a corner together. Ellen slipped down the corridor and poked an eye around it. The two men were deep in conversation some yards down a long corridor. The heavy set man was wearing an expensive tuxedo and watch. He looked like he was wealthy and very used to it. He also looked like the kind of man who didn't take no for an answer. Ellen decided there was something very familiar about him. She had seen him before but she couldn't remember where. Since they were too far away to overhear their conversation Ellen decided not to risk discovery. She slipped quietly back to the ladies room and inside.

Some minutes later she was back at the party accepting another glass of sparkling cider from a wandering waiter and looking for the mysterious man. She sighted him and kept him in sight as he moved through the crowds. He greeted many people, knew more than a few by name and shook many hands. Whoever he was he seemed to know everyone.

Ellen also managed to get close to the Attorney General and listen to bits of conversations he had with various bureaucrats and political contributors. Ellen was forced to admit that he was intelligent and very slick in his handling of people. Perhaps too slick; she could see how Steve might have fallen under this man's influence.

By eleven o'clock Ellen was ready to leave. She could not even look at another glass of cider and she was getting tired of having her feet trampled on by clumsy dancers. Her quest for information on Steve had largely failed. She had met no one who worked directly with him or was a good friend. The only person she was sure would have information about him was the Attorney General himself and she hesitated to approach him. As the highest law enforcement officer in the state it would not be good to arouse his suspicions. He had direct influence on police forces at all levels in the state of California. As she picked up her stole and made for the door it occurred to her that he would be in a perfect position to quash any serious investigation into Steve's death.

Once her car was brought around Ellen drove sedately away. She cruised aimlessly through Sacramento for a time to make sure that she wasn't being followed. Certain that no one was following her, she drove to Steve's apartment building. The apartment building was still quiet. A few lights showed in windows but most were dark at this hour. Ellen drove a few more blocks until she found a dark alley behind a retail store. She pulled the car into it and turned off the engine. It was the work of a few minutes to remove her formal dress and change in to her long black gown. She added a white cape. Her gun and hypo went into their holders and her black mask went into a hidden pocket of the cape.

She drove back to Steve's building and boldly parked across the street. She was taking a chance but she felt it was a small one. It was doubtful that the men she had encountered the night before would be expecting her to return. Undoubtedly they had searched the apartment and either found what they were looking for or not. Either way it was unlikely they would return. She left the car and crossed to the front door. It was locked but it was the work of only a minute to pick the lock and slip into the dim lobby. All was quiet as she located the stairs and climbed quietly to the third floor, as she did, she slipped her black mask over her face.

At Steve's door she used her pick and quickly gained admittance. She looked up and down the hall before entering. All was silent. She flipped on the overhead light. The living room had been thoroughly searched. The sofa and chair had been turned over. The cushions had all been slit open; stuffing was everywhere. The rug had been turned back as well. She turned off the light and moved to the kitchen. It was the same there. Drawers and cabinets had been opened their contents scattered across the floor. As she turned off the light and moved to Steve's office the Domino Lady mused about the noise such a search must have made. Yet the police hadn't shown up; interesting.

Steve's office was the same. His desk had been ransacked and the files in his cabinet had been scattered across the floor. All of his personal books had been examined and tossed on the floor. It looked like the law books had been moved around and examined superficially as well. Domino Lady bent over and began sorting through the pile of books. It took a minute of searching but finally she came up with the thick volume of Shakespeare she had seen before. She took the book to the desk and opened it up. Quickly paging to *Romeo and Juliet* she turned the pages one at a time looking for hand written notes in the margins or underlined lines. When she came to the quote her breath caught for a moment. Where the pages met near the spine a small section of page had been cut or torn and taped back in place with clear tape. She peeled back what was revealed to be two or three thicknesses of page glued together revealing a small area of the page that had been hollowed out to a depth of an eighth of an inch. In this small cavity was glued a brass key.

The Domino Lady reached for it, then stopped and drew her hand back. Instead she snapped the book closed and moved through the apartment turning off lights as she went. When she reached the hall she found it empty. She closed the door behind her and slipped toward the stairway. There was no one on the stairs and the lobby was still empty. She paused on the door step long enough to remove her mask before casually crossing the street to her car. Moments later she was driving quietly away.

Back at her hotel Ellen crossed to the elevators nodding at the sleepy night manager and had the operator take her to her floor. Once safely in her suite she opened the book and removed the key. A quick examination showed the number 32 engraved on the key in large numbers. Ellen had seen keys like it before, it was the kind of key used in public lockers. Making up her mind she moved to the bedroom and began packing.

The night manager was a bit surprised that Ellen was checking out so early but he was still very polite as he settled her bill. The last thing she did before leaving was to ask directions to the bus terminal. Soon she was zipping through the empty late night streets.

The bus terminal was quiet but not closed. There were a few people dozing in the waiting room and a janitor listlessly mopped the floor. No one paid Ellen any attention as she crossed the lobby to the storage lockers near the restrooms. She had the key in her right hand as she counted down the lockers. She stopped in front of a row of lockers and frowned. Number thirty two already had a key in the lock. When she reached out and pulled on the locker door, it swung open. The locker was empty.

Ellen pocketed the key and marched across to the counter where a lone clerk was reading a magazine. As she reached the counter he looked up expectantly. Ellen smiled and quickly asked for directions to the train station. He frowned but quickly gave them to her. Ellen thanked him and left.

Ten minutes later Ellen was entering the train station. Although a little busier than the bus terminal it was still quiet at this time of night. Ellen had little trouble finding the bank of lockers. When she counted down the numbers she quickly discovered that number 32 was locked. She took a breath and fitted her key in the lock. It fit. She turned the key and opened the door. Inside was a large, bulky manila envelope. As Ellen lifted it out, she could tell from its weight and feel that it contained a large amount of paperwork. She tucked the envelope under one arm and strolled out of the station to her car. Before starting up she looked around but could see no one taking any interest in her.

She pulled out on the street. Not far away she found an all-night filling station. She had the attendant fill her tank as she glanced through the envelope's contents. There were copies of government contracts, copies of schedules, file cards and copies of various memos and other letters on government stationary. This certainly was Steve's secret file. As the attendant finished, Ellen stuffed everything back into the envelope and secreted it under her seat. She paid the attendant and asked directions to Highway 99. The sooner she got safely home the better.

It was the kind of key used in public lockers.

Two days late Ellen, in comfortable silk pajamas lounged on the sofa in her expensive apartment. Her legs were curled under her and in one hand she held a champagne glass filled with orange liquid. In the other hand she held a letter sheaf of official looking documents. She sipped her champagne and orange juice and frowned as she read some government construction contracts. She was not a trained attorney but the terms seemed awfully favorable to her untrained eye. This was one of many documents that she had gone over in the last two days. She did not recognize the company involved but she made note of the name to check it out later, along with the other companies she was seeing in these government contracts.

She put down the contract and picked a sheaf of papers. They seemed to be copies of someone's appointment calendar. The same name was circled repeatedly on different days for meetings or phone calls. Ellen sat up straight. The name was Noah Crane. Crane was a well-known California business man. It was said he had made his original fortune in bootlegging on the East coast. He had come west a couple of years before and was cutting a wide path through the California business community. He had made many widely publicized gifts to charities and invested in infrastructure and public projects. In addition it was said he owned interests in varied construction companies.

Any rumors of his early questionable business practices and partners had been rapidly submerged by his contributions to charity and public works. All in all he was rich, powerful and well connected. More importantly though, he was the man Ellen had seen talking privately with the Attorney General. What was their connection? She dove back into the pile of documents. A few minutes later she found a "To Whom it May Concern" letter that had somehow gotten mixed in a stack of documents. It stated that Steve suspected that Crane had bought his way into the Attorney General's favor. Steve believed people in the AG's office were deliberately protecting him from investigation in exchange for campaign contributions and cash payouts. It also stated that Steve believed the AG had plans to run for governor in the next election with Crane's backing. Ellen shook her head when she had read it. Too bad she hadn't found this first. It explained a lot.

Ellen spent the rest of the day going through the documents. Now knowing what she was looking for helped. By the time she had gone over everything she could see a definite pattern of contact between Crane and the Attorney general and others in the AG's office. She could also see that Crane had huge but largely unseen dealings with governments at many levels. She needed to follow up on the companies associated with him but she would not be surprised to find Crane owned or partially owned them, perhaps through proxy owners. What she had not found was definite evidence of payoffs to anyone in government.

Ellen picked up the final sheet. Steve had been researching Crane's organization before he died. He had included a partial list of Crane's above board business, addresses and phone numbers. It was a place to start. Ellen was appalled at Crane's influence and she was also sure that he had been behind Steve's death. She also suspected the Attorney General's office had also been involved somehow; perhaps directly, perhaps in the cover up. Either way, tomorrow Ellen would begin the process of bringing justice to Crane and any crooked politicians on his payroll. She stood up to stretch. For now she would change and treat herself to a nice dinner while she planned her campaign.

Ellen began the next day. She went to the library and the offices of the *Times* looking up articles and references on Noah Crane. Using the list of companies that Steve had put together she began visiting the companies he was thought to own or control. She even drove past his large Orange County mansion. Carved out of an orange grove that he had bought up and plowed under, it was a masterpiece of marble, brick and stone. Set on acres of landscaped property it positively oozed money. She even put out feelers to some of her more socially active friends hoping to gain admittance to his social circle and learn more about his personal life.

The days rolled by. As she became familiar with his life Ellen realized just how many ties he had to political and business leaders. Some of this had been hinted at in Steve's files and it was easy enough to confirm. There was plenty of evidence to show Crane's close ties to the Attorney General and throw some suspicion on their relationship but that was a far cry from proving that he was on Crane's payroll. At the thought of payrolls Ellen got an inspiration. There had been no paper trail of payoffs by Crane but Steve had thought here must be. The question was; where would she find something like that. Records like that would certainly be kept in a secure location. A safety deposit box perhaps? No, Crane would want easier access than that. But Crane wouldn't keep his own books would he? No, he would have a professional bookkeeper or accountant.

Ellen dug through the notes she had made over the last few days. There it was. Crane's financial records were handled by the firm of Hansen &

Young CPAs. Ellen reached for the telephone. Five minutes later she had an appointment the next day to discuss her late husband's fortune. She smiled to herself. She would no doubt make an attractive widow.

As Ellen leaned back and lit a cigarette the phone rang. It was her friend Cindy. Cindy was an up and coming actress contracted to Columbia who had recently landed her first decent part in a movie. A producer at the studio where she worked had gotten her an invitation to a big party thrown by Noah Crane. She knew that Ellen wanted to meet Crane and wanted to know if she was busy on the coming Saturday. Ellen was certainly available. She made arrangements to pick her friend up and rang off. It certainly looked like things were coming together.

The next day found Ellen entering a high rise building in downtown Los Angeles. She was dressed all in black; dress, stockings, hat and veil. The clothing did little to disguise her figure and blonde hair though. It was just as she had thought: she made a stunning widow. The building directory showed her that Hansen & Young took up two floors in the building. Apparently they were a well-respected firm. As she crossed the lobby Ellen took careful note of her surroundings. After all, the Domino Lady might end up paying a late night call on Hansen & Young. One never knew.

At the Hansen & Young office she was greeted politely by a receptionist and shown to a seat. After a short wait, she was introduced to a prosperous looking, middle aged man with glasses who introduced himself as Ernst Young. He shook Ellen's hand and ushered her into an expensively furnished inner office. When they were comfortably seated he inquired, "First, let me extend my condolences Mrs. Montague. You have my sympathies. May I offer you some coffee?" Ellen declined and he continued, "Now, how may we help you Mrs. Montague?"

Ellen replied from under her veil, "Thank you Mr. Young. As I told your secretary my late husband has left me his entire business portfolio. I'm afraid I'm not too good with figures and I don't understand exactly what assets he has left me. What I need is someone to sort things out and advise me on exactly how to manage his...now my assets."

Ellen saw Mr. Young's expression change from one of polite interest to one tinged slightly with greed as she spoke. She had been counting on just that reaction. He leaned forward, "Mrs. Montague I'm sure that your husband must have had competent accountants. Perhaps they . . ."

Ellen cut in smoothly, "Yes, he did. I'm looking for a firm of my choosing that I can trust to give me good advice. Are you that firm?"

Mr. Young smiled confidently, "Of course we'll be glad to help you in any way we can. We have the best accountants available on staff."

Ellen smiled to herself. With the hook set, she now began reeling the fish in, "So I have been told. Is it true that you handle all of Noah Crane's accounting?"

Young hesitated for a moment, "Yes we do handle all of Mr. Crane's accounting and advise him on his investments."

Ellen caught his hesitation but pressed on as if she had not, "Good. I'd like to speak to his head accountant. If he's good enough for Noah Crane that's the man I want doing my accounts."

Young leaned back in his chair and cleared his throat, "Well, that's going to be difficult."

"Oh. How so?"

"Well, up until a few months ago Felix Harlech was in charge of the team handling Mr. Crane's accounts. I'm afraid though he is no longer with the firm."

Interested Ellen probed gently, "Really? He wasn't discharged was he?"

"Oh certainly not, as it happens he left to work personally for Mr. Crane."

"Noah Crane hired him away from you...really? That certainly says something about his abilities. What sort of work is he doing for Crane?"

Young looked somewhat uncomfortable at the direction of the conversation. He cleared his throat, "Um, I'm not exactly sure of the nature of the work Harlech is doing for Mr. Crane. However it is strictly personal in nature. We still manage the bulk of Mr. Crane's accounting and investments."

This was very interesting, Ellen thought to herself. Felix Harlech might bear a closer look. Still she had to play out her hand. She smiled at Young and said in a friendly tone, "Well, it's too bad that he has left but I'm sure that your firm is up to helping me manage my accounts. Can you tell me more of your firm?"

Young certainly could and did, at length. He expounded on the qualities of his firm long enough that Ellen interrupted him to ask for that coffee after all. It was quickly brought by an assistant who was anxious to look at her legs as well as offer her cream and sugar. Ellen asked the right questions in all the right places and soon had talked Young into taking her on a tour of the office. During their tour, Ellen asked lots of questions about the firm while taking careful note of exits, office locations and windows. It was always wise to be prepared.

They finished their tour with Ellen being introduced to the other partner Fred Hansen. He also went out of his way to be charming to the widow Montague. Later as Ellen was shaking hands with the partners and assuring them they would be hearing from her she speculated on how popular rich, grieving widows seemed to be. Once in her roadster she removed her veil and shook out her rich blonde hair. Being a widow had worked for the accountants. Now she had to become someone who would attract the attention of Noah Crane on Saturday.

Saturday came quickly. Ellen had spent the intervening days productively. In addition to researching Felix Harlech and finding out his work schedule and where he lived, she had found time buy a new maroon gown for the party that she was sure would turn heads. Other than careful choice in jewelry and perfume Ellen's preparations were easy. She wasn't planning on any extra-curricular activities that evening and so carried nothing more incriminating in her purse than lipstick. This was intended to be strictly a reconnaissance mission. She planned on meeting Crane and sizing him up as well as scouting the layout of his home. Chances were his private ledgers were secreted somewhere in the mansion itself.

Ellen was driving on Saturday evening. It seemed that Cindy's date did not own a car. At just before eight Saturday evening she pulled up in front of Cindy's apartment complex. It was a newer two story u-shaped complex in faux Spanish colonial style. The center of the U was a very nice garden with fountain. Cindy had moved here a few months before and Ellen reflected that her "private career counseling" with a certain studio producer must have done her some good. Following the walkway past the fountain Ellen was quickly knocking at Cindy's door. It was immediately jerked open by her friend. Cindy was a thin and very attractive. When you looked at her the word vivacious immediately came to mind. As Ellen gave her a hug she also reflected that Cindy's red hair and friendly personality didn't hurt either her career or love life.

After their greetings Cindy pulled Ellen by the hand into the living room. She gestured to the man just standing up from the sofa, "Ellen, I want you to meet Bob Heinlein my date. Bob, this is Ellen Patrick."

Ellen stepped forward and offered her hand to the handsome young man who smiled at her, "I'm charmed Miss Patrick."

"Please, call me Ellen." As she took his hand she sized Bob up. He was perhaps a little younger than her. He wasn't particularly tall but he was trim and fit. His dark wavy hair, firm chin and open smile showed why Cindy was dating him.

He replied, "And I'm just Bob. Thanks for offering us a ride to the party. You saved me from borrowing a car."

Before Ellen could ask the question, Cindy cut in, "Bob is a naval officer. He's stationed here on the uh…what was your ship's name Bob?"

He answered Cindy but continued to look at Ellen, "The Lexington, she's moored here in San Pedro."

Ellen had heard of the *Lexington*. She and her sister ship the *Saratoga*, commissioned recently were said to be the biggest ships in the navy. Nodding, Ellen imagined him in uniform and decided he looked every bit like a naval officer. She smiled at him and said, "The Navy, that sounds interesting. You must have lots of stories."

Cindy nodded enthusiastically, "Oh yes, Bob says the *Lexington* was in Washington this winter supplying power to all of Seattle, Isn't that right?"

Modestly the young officer replied, "Well, technically it was just the city of Tacoma. We hooked up to the city's power grid to help out during the drought last winter."

Ellen looked at her watch, "I'd love to hear more stories but I think we'd better get going or we're going to miss the party."

Cindy pooh-poohed this but still reached for her wrap. Soon all three young people were in Ellen's roadster laughing and looking forward to a casual, evening of fun: At least two of them were.

A half hour later they were pulling up in front of Crane's imposing mansion. The extensively landscaped grounds were lit up as was the building itself. Soon Ellen was entering the house on one of Bob's arms with Cindy on his other. Crane's home was as impressive inside as out. There were a lot of people present eating, drinking and chatting in small groups. Within minutes Ellen recognized several local officials and quite a few city business leaders. In addition Cindy pointed out several important men from the movie industry.

After grabbing champagne from a passing waiter the three mingled. As she sipped Ellen decided that prohibition was not in effect here tonight despite more than a few public officials in attendance. Cindy gravitated naturally toward some of the movie people and Ellen followed along, all the while looking for a way to slip away to explore the house. She also kept an eye open for Crane She really wanted to meet him and take his measure personally.

When the opportunity presented itself, she excused herself and went to look for a restroom. She left the ballroom, turned into a wide hallway and started opening doors. The first was a large library. Slipping inside she closed the door behind her. Three walls were covered by floor to ceiling bookshelves. Two large windows on the fourth side looked out on the illuminated garden. Even now Ellen could see two couples strolling across the grass. Several comfortable armchairs were scattered about the room. With drapes open there was neither time nor privacy to search for hidden safes but she marked its location and returned to the hall. The next door down opened onto a room dominated by a large billiard table. Four men in evening clothes were playing but stopped to look up as Ellen entered. She tried to look surprised and confused, "I'm sorry I'm looking for the powder room. Please excuse me." She quickly exited and decided to return to the main room. It wouldn't look good to be gone for too long.

She went to the bar and ordered a glass of ginger ale before looking for Bob and Cindy. She soon spotted them talking to a prosperous looking man. She sauntered over to join the little group. As soon as she did Cindy introduced her to Peter who it turned out was a movie producer for Columbia and Cindy's patron who was "assisting" her career. While listening to movie gossip she spotted her target out of the corner of her eye. Crane, impeccably dressed in a tuxedo was talking to a man she recognized as a city councilman from Los Angeles. She was figuring a way to get an introduction when she caught Crane eyeing her, or rather their group. Ellen watched covertly as he excused himself and headed their way.

She tried to look casual as Crane strode up to their little group. He held a drink in his hand as he spoke confidently, "Well, Peter you must introduce me to these beautiful ladies."

The producer turned to Crane and smiled, "Hello Noah. It was kind of you to invite me. Allow me to introduce you to Cindy Brooks. Cindy is one our future stars." Cindy held out her hand and Crane gallantly bent over and brushed the back of it with his lips, "Enchanted." Cindy blushed while young Heinlein looked on with amusement. Ellen tried to look impressed as Crane turned to her, "And you lovely lady are…?"

She held out her hand, "Ellen Patrick, Mr. Crane. Thank you for the lovely party." He repeated his performance on Ellen's perfectly manicured and outstretched hand and said, "Thank you for coming, and please call me Noah." He turned and exchanged handshakes with Heinlein and made small talk. He was casual but Ellen noticed immediately that he had eyes only for Ellen and Cindy. So…she thought to herself, he's a ladies man. Not surprising, men of power often were. He was tall and although not handsome had the dominating presence of a man used to giving orders and having them obeyed.

When she had an opening she addressed Crane, "Noah, you have such a lovely home. How large is it?"

Acknowledging the admiration he said proudly, "There are twenty four rooms, counting the bathrooms of course," he added with a smile. Cindy added eagerly, "And how many bathrooms are there?"

"Five, actually." There was a chuckle from everyone present.

Noting that Crane had been keeping a careful eye on her ample bosom Ellen took a chance, "It is a wonderful home. I'd love a tour." While she spoke she gave him her biggest smile. Crane replied, "Why I'd be happy to. Let's get another drink and I'll show you around." He led Ellen toward the bar. Cindy gave her a knowing smile as she left following Crane.

With fresh glasses in their hands Crane then led her down a hallway past the main stairs, "Down this way are the solarium, the music room, billiard room and library."

"I'd love to see your library" Ellen said putting a hand on Crane's arm. He smiled and led her to the library and opened the door for her. Ellen pretended surprise at its size, "My, what a fine collection of books and it's so peaceful here. Is this where you do your thinking?"

Crane sipped his champagne, "Actually I spend more time in my study when I'm reading."

Ellen looked around, "Oh…is that next door."

"Actually it's upstairs adjacent to my office and my…bedroom."

Ellen looked innocently at him, "Oh, just how many bedrooms are there?"

Crane stepped close to her, "There are six others and my suite, of course." Ellen was saved from a reply by the door opening. A uniformed servant stood in it, "Oh, here you are Mr. Crane. I'm afraid there's a telephone call for you."

Crane looked annoyed for a moment before replying, "Thank you James, I'll be right there." He turned back to Ellen, "You'll have to excuse me; perhaps we can continue our tour later."

Ellen tried to look disappointed, "Of course Noah. Think nothing of it." As he turned to leave the library she followed him telling him she would return to the main party to await him. Once safely back in the main room Ellen circulated. She found Cindy and Bob in deep conversation outside in the garden and decided not to disturb them. As she moved among the guests Ellen was deciding on how to make her exit. It would do no good to remain here. The house was far too large. It would take hours to search it properly. What she needed was more information on where Crane's confi-

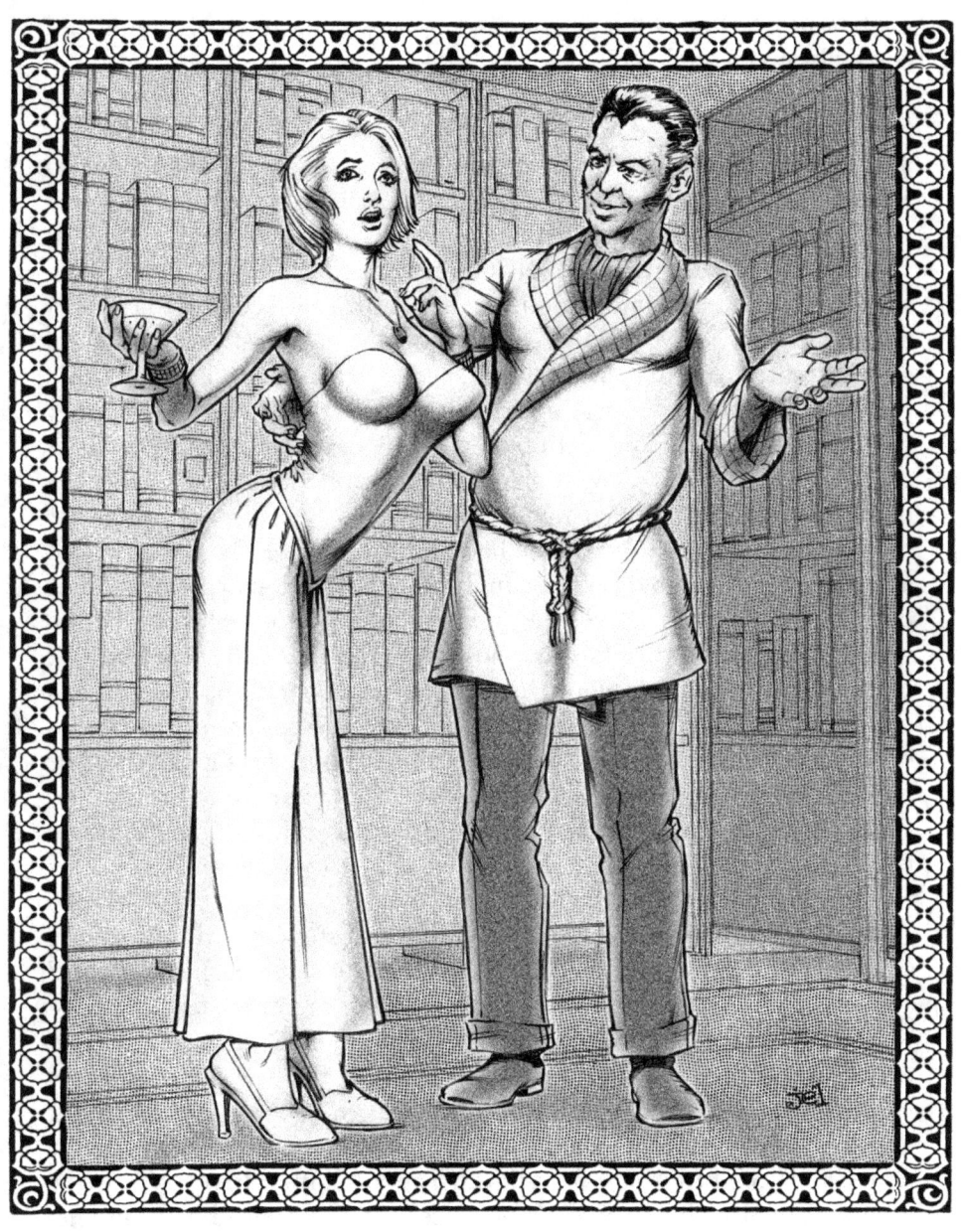

"Oh, just how many bedrooms are there?"

dential information would be hidden. She now knew the basic layout and could always return later.

She caught sight of Crane when he returned but managed to keep away from him as he worked his way through his guests. She found a servant and asked if she could use a telephone. The servant agreed and led her to a quiet room and indicated the instrument. Ellen thanked him and said that her mother was ill and she wanted to check on her. When he left Ellen picked up the receiver and pretended to talk on it for a few moments. Then she hung up and once more found the servant. She asked him to pass her compliments on to Mr. Crane and tell him she had been called away for an emergency. Careful to avoid Crane she found Cindy and Bob and made her apologies. They were very understanding and Cindy claimed that they could easily get rides home. Minutes later Ellen was wheeling her roadster down Crane's driveway. She didn't feel too bad. It looked like Cindy was in good hands with the charming Bob Heinlein.

The next day was Sunday. She had learned where Felix Harlech lived and had even driven by it. She again drove to his modest apartment building. Once there she parked and went to the front door. She buzzed the manager and asked for someone who did not live there. She kept him talking while she took a good look through the glass door at the lobby noting the elevator and stairway door. Afterwards she walked casually to the end of the block and around the corner. Seeing no one she slipped into the alley and took a good look around. Satisfied she returned to her car and drove home. She considered paying the bookkeeper a visit that night but decided to wait. She would need leverage to get what she wanted and for that Monday would be better.

Late the next afternoon Ellen was in her roadster down the road from Crane's expensive home. She was parked behind some bushes but could still see the mansion when standing next to her car. She knew that most week days Felix Harlech worked at Crane's mansion. Crane sent a car and driver to pick him up and return him home in the evening. The driver looked more like a bodyguard than chauffeur to Ellen's eye but that just added proof to her theory about Crane's bookkeeper. She waited patiently for over an hour before she saw a car turn out of Crane's driveway onto the road heading into town. Two people were in it. She hopped back into her car as it passed her and followed it toward the city. Within fifteen minutes she was sure they were taking the same route to Harlech's apartment as she had seen last week. She pressed the accelerator down and passed the car on a straight stretch of road. She had the top up and kept her head down as she did. Once in front of them Ellen pushed the car's speed up. She needed to arrive at their destination ahead of them.

With some aggressive driving Ellen reached Harlech's apartment with time to spare, so she hoped. She parked on the side street near the alley. In the car she checked her gun and her syringe before stowing them under her long white dress. She swung her cape over her shoulders and slipped on her black mask. Before she got out of the car the Domino Lady looked around, it was nearly dusk. The sun was just setting and shadows growing longer; she saw no one within sight. Slipping out of the car and wrapping her long black cloak around her white dress the Domino Lady glided down the alley.

In the gathering gloom she moved carefully to the back door of Harlech's building. It was locked but Domino Lady took but a quick two minutes to open the lock and move smoothly inside. The basement was dimly lit and she quickly located both the elevator and stairs. Ignoring the elevator she took the stairs quietly to the fourth floor. There she peeked into the hallway and saw that it was empty. Harlech's apartment was three doors down. Reaching under her dress she removed both her pistol and her syringe. The gun went into her right hand the syringe with cap removed went into her left. She waited hoping that no one would decide to use the stairway.

After a few minutes wait she heard the elevator door open and voices. She chanced a quick look into the hallway and saw the hulking form of the bodyguard looming over Harlech's smaller frame as the accountant unlocked his door. As the door opened the Domino Lady made her move. She swept down the hall and jammed the barrel of her small pistol against the back of the bodyguard's head, and commanded, "Don't move!" Harlech who had entered the apartment spun around. Seeing the masked form behind his guard he dropped his keys and his hands shot up. Domino Lady prodded the guard into the apartment and kicked the hall door shut behind her. The guard spoke, "Look lady you're making a big mis . . ." She prodded him hard in the neck with her gun and whispered harshly in his ear, "Take your gun out slowly and toss it across the room. He tried to stall, "I don't have a . . ." She cut him off, "Now!"

The guard stiffened in anger but reached slowly under his coat and came out holding a revolver. He tossed it onto the sofa. Domino Lady spoke harshly to Harlech, "You! Get down on the floor, face down, now!"

White faced, Harlech quickly complied. She then told the guard, "Okay, you go over there and tie him up. Use his belt and yours. Move!" The guard, mumbling under his breath did as he was told. When he had Harlech securely tied he turned toward her. His hard face glared at her. She gestured toward the bedroom door, "Okay get in there and don't try anything cute." Angrily he followed her instructions. When they were both in the bedroom she closed the door behind them and told him to face away. When he did she stepped quickly up behind him and jammed the syringe into his neck and pressed the plunger. It was filled with a fast acting drug that brought on unconsciousness in seconds. She pulled out the syringe as he clapped his hand to his neck and cursed. In another second his knees started to give way. As he swayed Domino Lady fired once downward into the bed. The shot sounded loud in the room but she knew it would barely be heard in the next apartment. The bodyguard collapsed hard to the floor with a loud thump.

Stowing away her syringe, the Domino Lady bent over the bodyguard and searched through his pockets until she found a small pen knife. Opening it she pricked one of his fingers and when the blood welled up she smeared it around on her left palm. Satisfied, she picked up her gun re-entered the living room. From the floor Harlech was twisting around trying to see what was happening in the bedroom. When the Domino Lady entered from the bedroom alone he went pale. Counting on the fact that he had heard the shot and the following thump, Domino Lady squatted down next to the bound accountant and silently held up her hand. If possible Harlech turned even a shade paler. She gave him a moment then spoke, "Now you know I mean business. If you don't want to end up like your bodyguard in the next room you'll tell me what I want to know. Understand?"

Harlech, clearly terrified, tried to answer but couldn't get the words out. Finally he nodded. The Domino Lady began the questioning, "I know Crane hired you away to do his confidential accounts. Where are the account books?"

It took the accountant a moment to get the words out but finally he croaked, "They're at Crane's house, in a safe."

Domino Lady nodded, "Where is the safe located?"

Harlech licked his lips, hesitated for a moment and whispered, "In the Study."

"Crane's study? Where is it? Upstairs somewhere?"

Harlech nodded, "Yes. I work in the study, its right next to his office and his bedroom."

"Alright where is this study: the front or the rear of the house?"

"The rear overlooking the garden."

Domino Lady nodded, "Now, where are the account books kept when you're not working on them?"

Harlech seemed to be getting his nerve back. His color was returning and he hesitated. The Domino Lady held up her left hand covered with now drying blood and shoved it in his face. She then hissed ominously, "You can be alive or dead when I leave. It's up to you." Sweat broke out on his face. He swallowed hard and whispered, "He'll kill me."

"I don't think so. After I leave, go to the nearest police station. Turn yourself in, they'll protect you. I think you're going to be very important to the D.A. by tomorrow."

Harlech looked surprised then he nodded. "Alright, the safe is hidden in a cabinet in the study. It's down low. Pull aside the liquor bottles and it's behind a wooden panel."

The Domino Lady nodded, "That's better. Now what's the combination to the safe?"

Harlech was defeated now. He barely hesitated before reciting tonelessly, "Left 37, right 53 and left to 22."

The Domino Lady stood up and crossed the room to the drapes. She jerked the cords down from the curtain rod. She then used them to replace the belt wrapped around his wrists. Leaving him she went into the bedroom. The bodyguard was still out cold and would be sleeping for quite a while longer. She repeated her work with the cord from the bedroom drapes. Once he was securely tied, she crossed to Harlech's dresser and removed two of his hand kerchiefs. One she used to gag the sleeping bodyguard while the other she used on Harlech. Before she left, she stooped over Harlech's gagged form and whispered, "The guard's not dead. He won't wake up for a while but he'll be okay." Harlech's eyes widened in surprise above his gag.

Leaving by way of the door, the stairs and finally the basement door The Domino Lady was quickly in the alley moving toward her car. Once inside she pulled off her mask and drove quickly away. She did not have much time. She had to move quickly before the guard got loose. Knowing she had only two or three hours Ellen pressed down the accelerator and the powerful car shot forward. Next stop Crane's mansion.

Less than a half hour later The Domino Lady was moving carefully across the darkened grounds of Crane's estate. The mansion had only been completed a couple of years before and although he had extensively landscaped the grounds; Crane had not yet gotten around to surrounding it with a fence or wall. The moon wouldn't rise until much later and thankfully the shadows were quite dark. Using those shadows as much as possible she gradually neared the house. Twenty yards from it she stopped under the branches of an orange tree. There were several cars parked near the entrance and the house was well lit on the first floor. Was Crane entertaining? If so, that would make things easier. She eased around to the rear of the house looking for a way to enter.

There several doors but they were all well-lit. Finally she decided on the darkened solarium. She ghosted up to its outside door. The glass door was locked but a few minutes work and it yielded to her lock pick. Inside the Solarium was mainly in darkness. An inner door was partially open and light and noise came from somewhere in the building. Gliding to the door she could hear distant voices and laughter. Probably from less than a dozen voices. Perhaps it was some kind of dinner party? The Domino Lady went through the door and turned away from the noise. She was in a familiar looking corridor. She moved quickly along it toward a back stairway that she had seen on Saturday. Past the billiard room and library she found it. She crept quietly up the carpeted stairs. Just as she reached the top she ran into a young woman wearing a maid's uniform entering the stairway from the upper floor.

The girl was shocked for a moment then opened her mouth to call for help. Fortunately the Domino Lady held her pistol in her hand. She thrust it forward and the maid's mouth closed quickly. "Turn around and don't move," the masked figure whispered. The maid complied. In seconds the Domino Lady had her syringe out. A quick jab and the girl quickly collapsed to the floor. Holstering her gun and syringe, the Domino Lady dragged the unconscious girl to a nearby door. It was unlocked. She dragged the girl inside, closed the door and flipped on the light. It was a guest bedroom from the look of it. Hefting the girl up, she laid her gently on the bed and flipped off the light.

Fifteen seconds later she was back in the hall moving to the hallway that paralleled the back of the house. There she started opening doors. They all seemed to be unoccupied bedrooms. Minutes later she opened the door of a more luxurious bedroom. It contained a huge four poster bed, a fireplace and lush carpet. It could only be Crane's bedroom. She slipped inside to get out of the hall and looked around. There was a connecting door on one wall. It led to a huge bathroom. She ignored it and turned to another connecting door on the opposite wall. This door led to an impressive office. It was paneled in dark oak and contained a desk that looked to be about half an acre in size.

Although tempted by the desk the Domino Lady kept on across the room to yet another connecting door. Opening it she turned on the light and found herself in a private study. There were comfortable leather armchairs, a wall of books, and a small table with a hooded light sitting on it. Nodding, she made for an oak side cabinet. It was waist high with a cigar case and a set of glasses on top. Bending down she opened the cabinet and saw several bottles of imported Canadian liquor. Squatting down she quietly moved them to the floor. It took a minute but she finally found the latch that let her swing open the wooden panel at the back of the cabinet. Behind it was a good sized safe. Praying that the frightened accountant had not lied to her, the Domino Lady twirled the dial to the numbers she had memorized. She turned the handle and there was aloud metallic click as the door opened.

Quickly she pulled the contents of the safe out onto the floor. There was a large wrapped bundle of large denomination cash, two leather covered check books, and a large envelope that contained a bunch of photos and negatives and three large account books. She sorted through everything quickly. The check books were tempting but bulky. The envelope was more interesting. The photos were of men and a few women some of them were in compromising situations. Others meant nothing to the Domino Lady but she was sure that they were all involved in blackmail in some way. She was torn. She couldn't carry everything. Finally she grabbed a handful of the photos and stowed them in a hidden pocket of her black cape. The rest of the photos went back in the envelope. She looked longingly at the cash and then reluctantly it went back into the safe along with the checkbooks and envelope. She would chance carrying the account books out with her.

Ready to depart, she pulled a black and white business card from the pocket in her cape and placed it over the remaining documents. On it in a fancy cursive scroll were the words, *Compliments of the Domino Lady.*

Closing up the safe and replacing the liquor restored the room to its normal appearance. With luck Crane wouldn't find anything missing before tomorrow. Moving to the corridor door she turned out the light and opened the door a crack. Down the corridor another woman in uniform was just coming out of what was probably a bedroom. She turned and entered another room. A maid turning down the beds? Perhaps. The Domino Lady wanted to leave quietly without risking another confrontation; every second she remained here was dangerous. She had her evidence and needed to leave now. Suddenly spying a telephone on the table she had an inspiration.

Grabbing up the receiver she dialed 0. When the operator came on the line she put a hysterical tone in her voice and shouted, "We need the fire department! The house is on fire!"

Calmly the operator replied, "Calm down ma'am. Where are you?"

The Domino Lady replied, "We're at Noah Crane's mansion. Hurry the fire's spreading fast!" She added the address and hung up quickly. Nodding to herself she thought, "That ought to do it." She glanced at her watch and thought for a moment. Then she picked up the receiver and dialed 0 once more. This time she asked for police headquarters. When she was connected she summoned up her best conspirator's voice and claimed there were two kidnap victims being held for ransom. She gave them Harlech's address and apartment number. Before hanging up she added that the men there were criminals. If Harlech changed his mind about going to the police this would help him along. Moving to the window The Domino Lady raised the sash and stood there listening. The night was pleasant and a slight breeze was blowing. She waited. Time drew out as she looked impatiently at her watch. Minutes later the breeze brought the sounds of sirens approaching. Grasping the account books she opened the hall door and looked out. It was empty. She slipped down the hall to the room where she had left the sleeping maid. She entered and pushed the door nearly closed. Listening at the crack she soon heard loud voices and could make out muffled sirens. Someone ran past; feet pounding along past the door. The sleeping maid wasn't a very big girl. The Domino Lady hefted the maid to her shoulder and grasping the books under one arm so her cape partially concealed them, she pushed out into the hall. She turned and moved quickly down the back stairs keeping her head low so that her long blonde hair helped conceal her mask. There were distant shouts and screams coming from the lower floor. As she reached it she turned toward the solarium. She could hear sirens more clearly now. She had almost reached the door to the solarium when she was nearly knocked down by a uniformed servant running the other way. He didn't stop or even look up as he ran past.

Once in the solarium it took less than a minute to cross the darkened room and let herself out into the side yard. Out on the darkened grounds she could see reflected red lights coming from around the front and could hear several angry voices shouting back and forth. The Domino Lady glided off into the darkness. She heard several shouts behind her but didn't stop to see if any of them were directed at her. She was breathing hard from the weight she was burdened under but still moved quickly. Finally in the shadow of an orange tree she gently laid the young maid on the ground. She would awake in an hour unharmed. Then she faded into the shadows carrying the precious account books with her. Once in her car she powered out onto the road. As she did she had to dodge a police car about to turn into Crane's driveway. She honked and waved as she sped past. She laughed heartily as she raced back into town.

Three days later Ellen Patrick lounged in her silk pajamas in her dining room. She lingered over her coffee and a cigarette as she re-read a headline article on the front page of the *Times*. It was an expose on Noah Crane. It stated that police were investigating Crane for extortion and the bribing of public officials. It further stated that after "extensive research" by *Times* reporters evidence had come to light of extensive payments to state and local officials as well as blackmail of both private and public figures. "Extensive research" my eye, Ellen thought as she snickered under her breath. She had anonymously delivered one of the ledgers and some of the black mail photos to *The Times* office late Monday night. Some research!

She had also seen to it that the police had gotten the rest of the evidence. It was certainly going to embarrass a lot of people and there would no doubt be many resignations and prosecutions but that was the price of corruption. The smile fell off of Ellen's face. She was pleased that she had exposed the people behind Steve's murder but it wouldn't bring him back. Still, perhaps she had gotten a little justice for her brave friend. Perhaps now he would rest a little easier.

The End

GOING TO THE WELL

*W*hen Ron Fortier put out calls for stories for a *Domino Lady* anthology last year I was all over it. The *Domino Lady* is a well-known character and I definitely wanted to be part of any new anthology. So I sent off a proposal and started in. Unfortunately I immediately had doubts. I've stated before that the masked avengers are my favorites and I write a lot of action and adventure stories that are filled with gunfights, chase scenes, fires and explosions. So it suddenly hit me that the Domino Lady was a totally different kind of character. She fights crime and exposes corruption certainly but she doesn't use twin automatics or her two fists. That's just not her style.

Instead the *Domino Lady* and her alter ego Ellen Patrick depend more on brains and planning. She has a gun and her trusty hypodermic syringe but her main weapon is her beauty and feminine wiles which she uses to great effect in seducing and confusing her enemies. Infiltration and surveillance are two of her greatest assets. So faced with the fact that my stock in trade, action and violence, wasn't going to work for the *Domino Lady* I panicked a little bit. This didn't mean I couldn't write a story for her but it does mean that I agonized over it…a lot. First I worked and reworked my outline and then wrote and rewrote the story. I wanted to hit just the right tone for her adventure.

Those of you who have read *The Domino Lady Rolls the Dice* can judge for yourself how I did. I would be glad to hear from any readers who would like to let me know what they thought of it. In the end I think it came out well. Anyway, I was pleased when I finally sent the story off to Ron. But I had put a lot work and worry into it and I have to say I was relieved that it was finally off my plate and I could get back to chases, gun fights and action.

So, if my first *Domino Lady* was so tough to get right, why am I now writing another one? Good question. I believe the reason is that she is just such a different and compelling hero. I was glad to have written the first story but I thought it was an interesting interlude and now behind me. But instead, I kept coming back to her. I read a few new pulp stories about her from other authors and kept comparing them to mine. New scenes and story lines for her kept popping into my head. I found I kind of missed her. Finally, I gave in. I was just going to have to write another story for her.

There were no shortage of ideas running around in my head. The *Domino Lady's* specialty was exposing corruption in government and business with the occasional side trip of helping out friends that might have gotten themselves into trouble. My first story was about helping an old friend out. That left corruption as a possible topic. Not a problem. There was certainly enough of that floating around during prohibition. I must have taken all of five minutes to come up with a corruption idea. The details took a little longer to work out but the concept seemed doable. With an idea firmly in mind I cranked out a detailed outline in double quick time.

The actual writing of *The Domino Lady's Justice* went much faster than my first story about her. In fact I felt right at home writing her. The truth is that writing about a beautiful woman flirting and infiltrating various bad guys and their nefarious plots can be a lot of fun. And what a *Domino Lady* story may lack in fights and car chases it certainly makes up for in beautiful gowns, silk pajamas and luxurious bubble baths. Plus there is just enough sneaking around in the mask to keep things lively. This is the formula I used in both my Domino Lady stories and I am pleased with both of them. I hope you like them as well.

So, will I write any more Domino Lady stories? It's kind of hard to tell. There is such a thing as going to the well once too often but I don't think that's the case here. There are definitely more stories of the glamorous, masked lady up my sleeve. The answer is more likely to depend on whether Ron has plans for additional Domino Lady anthologies. If he does? I imagine I'll be there. After all it's very hard to get a beautiful, buxom blonde out of your head. Especially one who has a mask and a gun.

Thanks for reading and we'll see you next time.

GENE MOYERS—studied European and Medieval history at the University of Oregon. He is also a U.S. Army veteran. He worked in the high tech industry for some time and ran a store front and internet hobby shop for several years.

An avid military gamer and role player, his favorite game was *Daredevils* a pulp based roleplaying game set in the 1930s. His love affair with the 1930s and pulps in particular stem from his first time reading a *Shadow* novel as a boy. Although interested in writing since a teen he did not turn to serious writing until 2000. He is the co-author of *GURPS Crusades* published by Steve Jackson Games. He has now written several stories for

Airship 27 including stories featuring *Ravenwood, The Purple Scar, The Moon Man, The Domino Lady and The Phantom Detective.* He has also written adventure stories for Pro Se Press anthologies.

When not working on various new pulp projects he is busy writing horror adventures for his swashbuckling character set in Colonial America. Gene currently lives in Beaverton Oregon with his wife and three lazy dogs.

THE DOMINO LADY'S TRIPLE THREAT

Brad Mengel

Ellen Patrick stretched and yawned, the band of sunlight peeked in through the blinds of her Wiltshire Blvd apartment gently waking her. Ellen reveled in the sensation of her red satin sheets, enjoying a rare morning free of appointments after her friend Eloise had cancelled their brunch. The life of a socialite was full of social engagements and philanthropic committees. That was tiring enough without Ellen's nocturnal activities under the guise of the Domino Lady.

While Ellen thrived on the constant adventure and danger, sometimes a girl just had to pamper herself. The gorgeous blonde decided that what she needed was a long soak in her bubble bath. Ellen rolled out of bed and pulled on the silk kimono she had bought during her trip to the Far East after her graduation from Berkeley. In fact it was the day that she bought the garment that she got the news that her father had been killed by the corrupt California political machine.

But the butter haired beauty was not going to think of such things as she turned on the water of her bath. Soon the bath was the perfect mix of hot water and soothing bubbles and the blonde bombshell slowly eased the robe off of her shoulders. Just as she was about to drop the robe and expose all of her alabaster skin, the tinkling of her phone intruded. Even though she had replaced the jangling bell for a more soothing ring, it was still irritating in these circumstances.

"Always the way." She thought as she wrapped the ornate silk kimono around her. "At least it wasn't a few minutes later."

"Hello." Ellen purred into the receiver, one never knew who was calling. The sultry tone was soon replaced by her natural voice as she recognized the caller.

"Uncle Dave!" She exclaimed happily. David Thornby wasn't her uncle but was given the honor as an old friend and colleague of Owen Patrick. Thornby was one of the few honest politicians in California and was now the Mayor of Berkeley. Rumor had it he was going to run for Governor.

"Ellen, my girl." came the avuncular voice, familiar from many dinner parties and family events of her childhood. "It's been so long since the last time I saw you. I bet you've shot up another foot."

It was a long running joke between the two; every time he saw her as a child he would make the same claim even if he'd seen her the day before. Ellen smiled at the memories. "Three years, and I've not grown an inch since then."

"Anyway, I know you're very busy. I see you in social pages of the papers all the time, so I won't take long." The older man started.

"I've always got time for you." Ellen replied.

"It does an old man's heart good to hear that. You might remember that your father and I were organizing an Anglo-American Bridge in Holmes Park here. I just wanted to be the first to let you know that it has finally gotten built and there will be a grand opening here in a week. Since it was your old man's idea, I'd like you to be here."

Ellen felt the tears threaten to well up in her brown eyes. "Of course, I'll come Uncle Dave. I can stay at …."

"Our place." Dave cut her off. "I won't hear otherwise. It's no problem and I know that Mary would love to see you."

Mary Thornby was like a second mother to Ellen during her time at Berkeley so Ellen was delighted to see the woman again. "I'll be there in a couple of days."

The end of the week saw the young woman packing for her trip, while she wasn't expecting any trouble she added a white dress, black cape and her special wrist bag. The bag was another souvenir from her trip to the Far East. When the neck was opened one way, all you could see was the typical items found in any socialite's handbag, lipsticks and the like. Opened the other way, the bag revealed very surprising contents: a needle containing a special fast acting anesthetic; a small automatic handgun and a domino mask…the signature look of the Domino Lady. Happy that she had everything she needed for her return to Berkeley for the first time in four years, Ellen called for a young man to collect her luggage and load it into her roadster.

Ellen hit the open road with the top down. She wore a pair of sunglasses to protect her eyes and as she drove her blonde hair streamed behind her. She looked the very image of the care-free socialite.

About eight hours later, Ellen arrived at the house she thought of as her second home. A familiar figure came out on the porch, in the past four years; the older woman had kept her figure but had gotten a few more grey hairs and wrinkles. The greeting Ellen got from Mary Thornby did nothing to dispel that notion that she had returned home. The older woman immediately wrapped Ellen in a hug and ushered her to the kitchen for a cup of coffee and to catch up. Ellen could see that behind the joy at seeing her surrogate daughter, the older woman was worried about something.

"Dave won't be home for a couple of hours, so that will give us girls time to catch up." Mary said as she poured the coffee. The chat started small with Ellen telling the woman she called Aunt about a recent lunch with Errol Flynn, although she deliberately omitted some of the more bawdy stories the film star told her. It was almost like Ellen had never been away.

As the afternoon turned into evening, Ellen noticed that Mary kept glancing at the clock with increasing frequency and the worry Ellen had noticed on her arrival became more and more prominent. By six, Mary was no longer pretending that she was listening to Ellen. When Ellen touched the woman on the shoulder, Mary jumped she was so caught up in her worry that it seemed that she had forgotten about Ellen.

"Aunt Mary, what's wrong?" Ellen asked.

"Oh dear, Dave should have been home an hour ago. He does get caught up in meetings, but he was so excited that you were coming that he wouldn't be this late. Did you know after he spoke to you on the phone the silly old duffer danced me around the room?"

Ellen could tell that the woman was trying to distract her, but she kept pressing. Over the past three years since the death of her father, Ellen had developed a sixth sense when the Domino Lady was needed. She had no official network of criminal informants instead relying on rumors and gossip. Luckily for Ellen, people had always opened up to her about their troubles. During her time at Berkeley, she was the agony aunt for her dorm. Now she was using her talents on her Aunt.

Mary sighed. "Dave doesn't know that I know this, but he received a threatening letter from the German-American Bund. I found it in the waste paper bin in his study. They told him that they would stop him from opening the bridge. I'm so worried that they've done something to him."

"I'm sure the Bund are just all bluster and bluff and Uncle Dave has been caught up in a meeting but I'll grab my handbag and drive out to see if he's okay."

Ellen went and collected her special handbag, she hadn't lied to the older woman but if she was wrong Ellen wanted to be prepared. The rest of the Domino Lady's outfit was in the trunk of her roadster. Ellen took the most direct route to City Hall and was soon rewarded with the sight of a car on the side of the road. Ellen threw the roadster into a U-turn and pulled up behind the car. Her headlights soon illuminated the rear of the black car and she could make out the name "Rosie" painted in white on the rear bumper.

The car was Dave's Model T Ford, Ellen remembered that when she was six during a visit with her father, Dave had brought the car home from the showroom. She had immediately named the car Rosie after her doll, the older man had painted the name on the rear bumper of the car. There was no mistake.

Ellen pulled a miniature flashlight from her bag and made her way to the Model T. She called for Dave a couple of times but the only response was the hoot of an owl. A quick touch of Rosie's bonnet told Ellen that the car had only fairly recently stopped as it singed her delicate fingers and marred her perfect complexion with a red mark.

Frowning, Ellen shone the torch into the body of the car. She suddenly feared the worst that she would find her uncle's dead body riddled with bullets. The thought of losing a second father figure to an assassin's bullet was almost too much to bear. When the circle of light revealed no blood, let alone a body, Ellen let loose the breath she had been holding.

As oxygen again coursed through her body, the blonde adventuress began to look for clues. Luckily, her footprints hadn't obscured the other tracks and she was able to follow them a few yards up the road. Near where the footprints disappeared, Ellen was able to find tire tracks. Hope surged in her breast as Ellen spotted taillights in the distance. It could belong to her uncle's abductors and if she pushed her roadster she should be able to catch them. Her tires spun dirt as Ellen again pushed her car to outrace an injustice.

The roadster was gaining on the vehicle in front of her. The lights disappeared in a dip of the road ahead of her. Ellen took advantage of being out of sight to switch off her own lights so that they wouldn't suspect being followed.

Ellen was surprised that once she cleared the hills she could no longer see the taillights in the distance. Immediately she turned on the lights and went back the way she came. As she returned down the road, her lights illuminated a concealed driveway. The plucky adventuress pulled over to the side of the road and parked the car behind a hedge. Ellen rummaged through the suitcase in the boot of her car and then with the skill and ease of a Burlesque Queen, Ellen Patrick took off her skirt and top. The cool breeze caressed her bare skin. She then pulled on the special backless white dress with the daring décolletage and halter neck. Her white kissable shoulders were soon covered by a theatrical black cape. Out of her handbag came the black silk domino mask that framed her brown eyes and the trusty little automatic pistol. Gone was the languid socialite; in her place was the young avenger of the helpless, the Domino Lady!

A soft summer breeze blew in from the coast, tousled Domino Lady's butter colored hair as she entered the driveway. Her torch illuminated a letterbox with the name of Braun, a German name she noted as she continued along the drive.

The daring young crime fighter was soon rewarded with the sight of a Daimler truck. For the second time that night, her fingers were burnt by bonnet of a recently driven vehicle. A grim smile crossed her face as she found confirmation that she was on the right track.

Slowly, Domino Lady opened the hood of the truck, careful not to make any noise. She flashed her light on the engine and quickly identified the distributor cap. As she reached for the component, Ellen sensed someone behind her. With the blinding speed born of years of training, Ellen pivoted on her left leg and kicked out with her shapely right leg. The tip of her shoe connected with the temple of the man attempting to sneak up on her, causing him to crumple to the ground like a puppet with cut strings. Miss Angelique, her ballet teacher would have applauded her flawless move and then frowned at the purpose it was being put to. A quick injection of her special anesthetic made sure that the Bundist would not be causing further interference, the young daredevil returned to her original intent of disabling the car, a few minutes and a fistful of wires later she had achieved her objective.

Domino Lady began her search for Dave Thornby. She moved with the silence of a ghost around the exterior of the house. She halted outside a lit window at the back of the house, with great care Ellen peered through the glass. It was a risk but one she had to take for the sake of the two people who were like second parents to her.

Much to Domino Lady's surprise she saw two men sitting around a kitchen table wearing the uniforms of the Nazi regime. It appeared that the American-German Bund were not just bluff after all. A third man come to the table, the reaction of the other two was suggestive that the newcomer was in charge. He poured himself a drink and sat down. The conversation soon degenerated into an argument and if she strained Domino Lady could make out enough of the words to know the men were talking in German. Luckily, Ellen Patrick's year in a Parisian finishing school before she started at Berkeley had taught her formal German, and a week's vacation in Berlin had taught her some of the more colorful and informal German phrases.

Domino Lady heard the word Thornby and her heart soared. She was in the right place! Ellen strained her ears and tried to capture more of what the men were saying. The Nazi sympathizers had kidnapped Dave Thorny to prevent him from opening the Anglo-American bridge. The gesture was largely symbolic to show the American people that they shouldn't be aligned with the English but rather with the strength of Nazi Germany. But not all of the Bund members felt this way. The smallest man at the table was arguing forcefully that symbolic gestures were not enough and that stronger actions were necessary. Domino Lady did not like the way the small ratty man with the little toothbrush moustache played with the knife cleaning his nails. The other two men at the table seemed to be of a more moderate view and tried to calm him. The daring young woman did not like the chances of herself or her uncle if the little man she had dubbed Adolph caught them trying to escape. She had to move quickly before the man she knocked unconscious was missed.

It was no sooner thought and Domino Lady was on the move. Like a big cat stalking its prey, Domino Lady circled the house searching for any means to enter. She quickly eliminated the back door that lead into the kitchen where the three Bundists were still arguing. To Ellen's dismay all of the ground floor windows were shut and she daren't try to open them in case she made a noise and alert the men inside.

Frustrated, Ellen leant against the large elm on the north side of the house. As Ellen looked at the branches, she noticed that one of the branches was close to an open window on the second story. A gleam of excitement lit up her eyes as she remembered there was a tree like this outside her window, a tree that more than once allowed the daring debutante to leave and reenter the house without her father being any the wiser. Those early lessons would come in handy now, as Ellen began to climb the tree. Slowly inch by inch, Ellen made her way up the tree carefully testing that each branch could hold her weight. The risks were a lot higher that when she was younger, then she only risked broken bones and a lecture from her father, now any misstep could result in the end of the career of the Domino Lady. As she climbed, Ellen was silently thankful that she was still wearing her flat driving shoes and not her usual French heels, this climb would have been impossible. With the grace and agility of a panther, Domino Lady leapt from the branch onto the window sill. Ellen gently eased into the room. She drew the torch from the pocket in her cloak and shone the light around the room. From what she could see it was an ordinary bedroom with a four poster bed. The room had woman's touch. The bedspread was a cheerful pink with red roses and the dressing table covered in beauty products were suggestive of there being a Fraulein Braun who was not around at the moment. Indeed it was likely that Herr Braun had sent his wife and children away while the Bund held Dave Thornby on the property.

Domino Lady gave a quiet sigh of relief and started her stealthy search of the house. She peered around the door and saw the hallway was clear. The next door opened as soon as Ellen turned the handle, she quickly ascertained that there was nothing out of the ordinary and there was no one in the room. The next door was locked and the masked woman pulled a bobby pin from her hair. She knelt down and began to manipulate the tumblers. Her perfect cupid bow lips were pursed in concentration until she felt the lock give and then she formed one of the lovely smiles that society photographers loved. The door opened and the light of her pencil torch showed a prone body on the bed. Ellen stepped into the room to examine the person better and was able to confirm that she had indeed found Dave Thornby. He was still breathing but they were not the rhythms of a naturally sleeping man but rather those of drug induced slumber. Dave had always been a big man and the last few years since she had seen him had added several pounds to his middle.

There was no way that the hundred and twenty pound Ellen Patrick would be able to lift the much heavier and larger man, she'd been barely able to lift J. Thomas Saint when she faced the Black Legion and Saint was a much smaller man. Dave Thornby would have to walk out. Ellen shook the older man, there was a slight grunt. There was no way he was going to wake in a hurry and even if he did wake up he would be in no fit state to assist in his escape. Domino Lady would have to clear the way first.

From her earlier scouting there were only three Bundists in the house with a fourth already taken out of action. Domino Lady made her way down the staircase. As her shapely leg descended onto the fifth step down, the stair made a loud creaking sound. Ellen stopped, her body tensed.

"Is that you Joseph?" called a voice from the kitchen in German.

After a minute with no response, the sound of a chair scraping against the floor reached the ears of the Domino Lady. Ellen crept down the stairs, reaching into the pocket of her cape. Another of her knockout syringes was ready for use. There was a small alcove in the landing in the middle of the stairs. Domino Lady pressed herself into this limited sanctuary and hoped to avoid exposure.

The commander of the trio soon came into view. He called for Joseph again and paused on the landing to listen for any further noises. At the last second, the Bund Commander heard a slight scuff behind him but it was too late. The short sting of the needle entering his skin was soon replaced by the oblivion of the fast acting drug of Domino Lady's own design. The impulse to yell a warning to his men was no match for the speed of the drug and only a gurgle passed his lips before he collapsed on the landing. The loud thud from the two hundred pound Bundist hitting the floor however performed much the same function alerting the two remaining Bund members to a problem. Two chairs scraped on the floor and two voices called for Heinrich.

The Domino Lady had faced worse odds before and triumphed but this was going to be a tight spot for the blonde bombshell. She retreated to the top of the stairs and listened. The cries of surprise told her they had found the unconscious man on the stairs.

"Clumsy oaf" declared a voice, "he never could handle his schnapps."

"Then let him sleep it off there," came the second voice which came from the man Ellen recognized as coming from the man she had dubbed Adolph.

"I have to check the prisoner soon and I'm not stepping over him. Help me get him to the chair over there."

Domino Lady had noticed that the stairs had ended in a sitting room earlier. What she had overheard was good news. If they needed to check on the prisoner that meant he was due to wake up soon and that only one of his captors would be coming up. Ellen silently padded down to the room where her uncle lay sleeping and carefully relocked the door. The young vigilante stood behind where the door would open and waited.

Her patience was soon rewarded by the sound of a key turning in the lock and the door opening. Domino Lady readied her third and final anesthetic needle and lunged for the man. It may have been luck or some sixth sense but the Bundist walking through the door stepped to the side. Instead of the needle plunging into the flesh of her target as had been the case every other time she had made this move, Domino Lady found the needle stabbing through the air. Her momentum carried her forward and she fell on her face. The needle drove into the floorboards and bent at an angle that made it impossible to use the needle. The laughter that came from the Bund member stung nearly as much as the pain Ellen was feeling in her knees and wrists.

"Heinz, I've caught the intruder. I can handle this. Go find Joseph," called the man in the room.

Ellen cursed herself mentally; she had fallen straight into the trap the

...this was going to be a tight spot for the blonde bombshell.

men had set her. Her keen ears detected the sound of a gun being cocked. Was this to be the end of the Domino Lady? If this was to be her final stand, Domino Lady was not going out cheaply.

At that moment, Dave Thornby came out of his stupor and sat up. The German sympathizer let loose one of the more volatile curses that had ever graced the Domino Lady's ears and turned his attention to his captive and pistol-whipped the politician back into unconsciousness.

It was a small reprieve but it was enough for a plan to form and Domino Lady to act. It was not much of a plan but acting was better than doing nothing and certain death. Domino Lady reached into her décolletage and pulled out the sap she had taken away from one of Herschel Donnowicz's henchmen a week ago. In desperation, Domino Lady threw the weapon at the Bundist. The blonde man recognized the danger a few seconds too late and the sap proved just as effective thrown as it was if used traditionally when it struck him on the temple. The blow however was too late to prevent his finger to tighten on the trigger of the Luger. A bullet struck the ground just a few inches away from the masked woman's head.

The Domino Lady slowly got to her feet. Her chest heaved as she gave a sigh of relief. It was one of the closest calls she had ever faced but there was no time to linger on how close she had come to death. The shot was sure to attract the attention of the fourth and final enemy in the house, the vicious little man she had dubbed Adolph earlier. No sooner had she thought that but Adolph came into the room. Luckily for both Domino Lady and Dave Thornby, the little man was not carrying a handgun. The thought that his fellow Bundists didn't trust the little man with a gun did little to comfort Domino Lady.

"I told them this was a stupid idea." Adolph said as he advanced on the adventuress. "Now I can do this my way. "

The little man had his knife poised to strike and Domino Lady had no time to draw her pistol. In a desperate move she whipped out her black cape like a matador. He reacted to the threat just as she hoped he would, stabbing into the fabric of the cape and tangling his knife.

Adolph was defenseless now. The Domino Lady's right fist lashed out and popped him right on the jaw. His head spun to the right as he sunk into unconsciousness. Ellen Patrick had never been so glad that she shared many of her father's interests including the pugilistic arts and bullfights.

With all of the threats out of commission, Ellen turned her attention to her uncle and she tried to wake him. He did not respond to her calling his name or shaking. Ellen even slapped him across his face with no response.

Ellen was starting to worry, she had no idea how long it would be before the first man she knocked out would be waking up. But it was these type of tight situations that the Domino Lady excelled, but it was Ellen Patrick who provided the solution.

A few days earlier she had been lunching with Mamie, one of the grand old dames of Hollywood, who was prone to fainting spells. Ellen had packed a vial of smelling salts into the everyday side of her handbag. She reached in now and waved the vial under Thornton's nose. The older man snorted and stirred. Domino Lady put the vial under his nose again, this time the salts did their job and Dave Thornton woke up. The older man was still groggy and Domino Lady led him to her car.

The Domino Lady looked at the groggy man sitting in her passenger seat and revised her original plan; even with the wind perking him up Dave Thornby was in no fit state to drive home. She drove past Rosie and straight to the Thornby house. Ellen lead her uncle to the swing seat on the front porch tucked one of her special black cards beside his pocket kerchief. After ringing the front doorbell, the Domino Lady returned to her car and drove to secluded location and changed back into her original outfit.

On her arrival back at the Thornby house a few minutes later, Ellen found a clearly relieved Mary Thornby fussing over her husband who was recovering from his ordeal.

"Thank God, he's home." Ellen said as she walked onto the porch. "I was starting to worry when I found nothing driving around." Ellen hated this part, lying to her family and friends but it was better that they didn't know about her extra activities.

"He was kidnapped by the Bund." Mary declared.

Dave groaned "Please keep it down. I have the worst headache." He reached for his pocket kerchief to mop his brow and pulled out the card. "Compliments of the Domino Lady."

Ellen could have sworn she heard her uncle mutter "it wasn't a dream" but she might have been mistaken, Dave looked strangely at Ellen as he told his wife to call the police to report his kidnapping.

It was only a matter of a few minutes before a pair of the detectives arrived at the Thornby house. The more senior detective introduced himself as Edgar Butler and his partner as Chas Faraday. Ellen looked the pair over. Butler was almost a stereotypical Irish detective, with a pot belly preventing his suit coat from buttoning up. He had doffed his brown derby hat and held it in his hands as he spoke with more than a touch of an Irish brogue when he asked questions and Ellen suspected that the bulge under his jacket was not a firearm.

Ellen paid special attention to Butler. The older cop, at first glance, appeared to be a dumb Irish flatfoot. His cry of "Faith and Begorah!" at the sight of the Domino Lady's calling card was a bit too over the top. Ellen's experiences with Roge McKane and Paul Cathern and her instincts told her there was more to the almost comical detective.

An instinct that was confirmed as Butler turned over the card and saw the address the Domino Lady had written there. Butler must have been quite a poker player as his reaction was muted, but he quickly called his colleague over for a conference. As much as Ellen strained she could not decipher the hushed conversation.

His partner on the other hand was a dashing young man about the same age as Ellen. Ellen looked over the handsome young officer. Unlike the more senior detective, his suit fitted perfectly on his broad shoulders and the slight bulge under his arm most likely was a firearm. His tousled brown hair gave him a boyish charm. Had the police looked like this while she was studying at Berkeley she might have gotten into, and out of, a lot more trouble.

However it was not just the handsome young officer that interested Ellen. Normally, once the Domino Lady had achieved her goal, she was gone before any official police involvement began. It was interesting to see the police in action close up.

Faraday asked the Thornbys if he could use their phone to inform Headquarters that they had arrived at the house. Dave waved his hand and the young detective went into the hallway to make his call.

Butler eased his bulk onto the couch near where Dave Thornby was sitting. After resting the derby on his knee he addressed the ailing man. "I can see that you've a headache to match some of my March 18 memories. Oh how I've prayed to Saint Pat on those days for some relief. And some hair of the dog 'taint really an option for you."

Mary patted her husband on the shoulder. "I sent for the doctor and he should be here soon."

"Now Mr. Mayor rest assured that the department is doing all they can to arrest those responsible." The detective continued, "So I'll keep this short and we'll get a formal statement in a couple of days when you feel up to it, but I just need a quick account of what happened from you."

Dave Thornby nodded his head, winced slightly, and began his story. There wasn't much to it; he'd been in a meeting with the budget committee which had run late. Knowing that Ellen would have already arrived, he had been driving home when a truck driving erratically had come up behind him. Dave had pulled his car onto the side of the road to allow the driver plenty of room to overtake. Rosie had no sooner pulled over to the side of the road that the truck pulled over in front of him and forced him out of the car and into the truck. He'd been injected with some drug and had fallen asleep. The next thing he knew he was sitting on his front porch holding The Domino Lady's calling card. He had a very dim recall of a woman in a mask fighting a man but it was hazy and if it wasn't for the card in his pocket he may have dismissed it as a dream.

Butler pulled out a cigar but a stern glance from the mayor's wife was enough to make him put it back and grab his notebook and pencil. As he was making notes, Faraday returned and whispered in the older detective's ear. Ellen's keen hearing picked up a couple of words and she was able to deduce that someone had been dispatched to the Braun house.

Faraday turned and noticed Ellen looking at him. He gave her a big grin and suggested to his superior that he interview Miss Patrick. Butler nodded his assent and the handsome detective ushered her into a nearby sun room.

Ellen elegantly perched herself on the two-seater sun chair and invited the detective to sit beside her. Ellen noticed that the detective's chest might have puffed out a little.

"Now Miss Patrick, don't you worry." The detective said, Ellen noticed that his voice had deepened a little since their introduction. "Your uncle will be safe, Detective Butler and I have arranged for a guard detail."

Demurely, Ellen responded, "I certainly feel safer knowing that you are on the case."

The young detective flashed her another smile and Ellen found herself almost hoping that there was more trouble so she could see more of the detective. Just then the phone rang, breaking the mood. Faraday leapt to his feet. "That might be headquarters. I'll be right back."

As soon as the detective was clear, Ellen padded across the room and listened at the door. The young detective's side of the conversation was not very enlightening but it did seem to be good news. Ellen soon returned to her seat and waited for Faraday to return.

The young detective returned to his seat and took Ellen's hand. He leant in conspiratorially and in hushed tones said "I'm not supposed to tell you this, but we sent a car out to the address on that card in your uncle's pocket. We arrested the three men responsible for the kidnapping; it looks like they were Bundists. Your uncle reported some threats from them a couple of weeks back. It's an open and shut case and we'll be able to put them in a jail for a long time. So you needn't worry, the threat is over."

Ellen smiled and put her hand on her chest emphasizing her generous curves. "I'm so glad to hear that. I was so worried that those horrid men might try again and that someone might get hurt."

"Look, if it makes you feel any better here is my card, you can call me at the station if you have any concerns." Faraday put his arm around the socialite's shoulders. Ellen did nothing to stop the man, but as much as she wanted to enjoy the detective's attentions, Ellen couldn't help thinking that there were four not three men at the Braun house. And she had a very bad feeling about which of the men had escaped.

Luckily for the blonde adventuress it was just then that the doorbell rang heralding the arrival of the doctor, so she didn't have to hide her worry. The young detective excused himself to answer the door and Ellen was able to follow the doctor and detective into the sitting room. Everyone assumed that the concern that the young woman wore on her face was for the health of her uncle, which was true only she was worried about his future health if Adolph was the man who escaped from the Braun house.

The doctor declared that his patient was none the worse for wear and a good night's rest was all he needed. With that declaration, Mary Thornby chased out the police and set about getting her husband to bed. Ellen bid her aunt and uncle good night and turned in herself, she was exhausted after the long day of excitement.

The next morning saw both Ellen and Dave Thornby up before the late rising Mary. After a hearty breakfast, Dave declared his intention to head to the office. Ellen tried to dissuade the older man but, much like her father, once Dave's mind was made up there was little that could shake the idea. Like many of his political rivals, Ellen eventually relented and offered to drive the older man to his office. The older man didn't wish to put his niece to any trouble but Ellen's argument that she was planning to head to town for a shopping spree and that Rosie had not been returned by the police had soon swayed the man. With one of the Bund still on the loose, Ellen was not inclined to let Dave Thornby travel alone. Especially, if her fears that the vicious man she had dubbed Adolph was the one to remain free.

The drive to the Town Hall was uneventful and as they pulled into the Mayor's car space, Dave pulled out his pocket watch.

"Eight-thirty on the nose." He declared. "I guess a late start can be forgiven after yesterday."

"I do wish you'd listen to Aunt Mary." Ellen said, "And stay home today."

"Nonsense, young miss," Dave replied. "The police assured us last night that those responsible have been arrested. I'm not going to let the Bund or any other criminal group stop me serving the people of Berkeley. I love your Aunt but she can be a nervous Nellie."

Ellen couldn't disagree with him on that. "You're probably right, but you've had a hard time."

The old man laughed. "When your Dad and I were pledging, we went through worse than that. There was one time…" Thornby cut himself off realizing that particular story might not be suitable to tell Owen Patrick's daughter.

To cover his awkwardness Dave Thornby got out of the car, circled around the car and opened the door for Ellen. "Come in, I'll show you around."

Ellen smiled a beatific smile as she stepped out of the roadster, "And tell me about the misspent youth of Owen Patrick and David Thornby?" she teased.

Thornby laughed. "Not in front of my staff." But he launched into a story about their glory days on the college football field, which was far tamer than the one he started a few moments earlier. Ellen and Dave were laughing at the story of Owen Patrick losing his pants during a tackle and running the length of the field in his boxers when they got to the Mayor's office.

"My secretary should be here by now." Dave frowned as the door handle refused to turn. Dave fumbled in his pockets for his keys.

"I'm so sorry Mr. Mayor." A deep masculine voice echoed along the hallway and sent tingles along Ellen's spine. "I was delayed by a flat tire. "

"That's alright Brent." Dave replied. "I just got here myself."

Ellen turned to see the secretary. In her head she expected the secretary to be a man of the same vintage as Dave so she was surprised to see a man in his early twenties. He was carrying his light grey jacket and had his sleeves rolled up to reveal muscular forearms. Traces of dirt and grime marked his hands and face. His sun bleached blonde hair was messed up and drooped over his left eye.

"I'll let you and your niece into the office and then go clean up." Brent said as he pushed his fringe back and left a greasy smudge on his forehead "Those letters are on your desk and if you sign them soon I can get them in the early mail."

It was the work of a moment and Ellen found herself sitting in a comfortable leather chair watching her uncle signing several pieces of correspondence. Brent soon joined them, this time looking more presentable, his face cleaned and unruly mane of hair tamed. As the secretary collected the letters, Dave made more formal introductions.

"Brent, as you've already worked out this young lady is Ellen Patrick. Ellen, this is my secretary Brent Richards."

"Lovely to finally meet you." Brent said. "The mayor has done nothing but talk about you for the last week."

The young man gave her a smile showing his perfect white teeth. It was an easy smile that sent a shiver along Ellen's spine. Ellen had spent her life around politicians and she could see Brent was destined for political life and a much larger role than secretary to a city mayor. The Domino Lady was working hard to expose and destroy the corrupt political machine that ruled California and had sent an assassin's bullet taking away her father. Knowing that men like Brent were being groomed to be the future gave Ellen hope that one day she might be able to take off the Domino Lady's mask for good.

"It's been a pleasure to meet you too." Ellen smiled back. "It looks like you both have a lot of work and there is the most delightful little boutique I used to buy all my dresses when I was studying that I have to visit. Uncle Dave, I'll be back at noon to take you to lunch." Ellen kissed the older man on the cheek.

Ellen made her way through the Town Hall and spent the morning revisiting her old stomping grounds. The staff of the boutique remembered her and Ellen left with a stylish red and black dress. At the beauty parlor, she discovered that her stylist, Cécile had left to marry and was now the mother of two little boys.

After her pleasant trip down memory lane, Ellen returned to the Town Hall. Dave Thornby made the excuse that he was far too busy to stop for lunch and he had ordered a hero sandwich from a nearby deli but Brent was due his lunch break and could take their restaurant booking. Dave handed his secretary a fifty to pay for the meal.

Not that Ellen was adverse to spending time with the handsome young man, but she suspected that her uncle was trying to play matchmaker.

Ellen had not given much thought to what would happen at the end of crusade. Could she settle down as the demure and proper politician's wife like her mother and Aunt Mary?

Of course, Ellen thought to herself, I'm getting ahead of myself. If Brent suspected that she was thinking of marriage he might run in the opposite direction.

"Uncle Dave, I'll be back at noon to take you to lunch."

The young couple walked to the car.

"My car is just here." Ellen said as they exited the building. "And I have a functional spare."

Brent flashed another of his smiles as he climbed into the passenger seat. "You have me there. My car is at the mechanics around the corner. After lunch I was planning on picking it up. If I could trouble you to drop me there on the way back."

"I think that can be arranged." Ellen said as she pulled into the traffic.

The meal at the restaurant was excellent and Ellen relaxed enjoying herself. All too soon it was over and they had to return to the Town Hall.

In the car, Brent turned to Ellen. "I have to confess something. The old man isn't that busy."

Ellen laughed. "I had a feeling that was the case and he was indulging in some match making."

Brent actually blushed. "That might have been part of it but he likes to have a siesta after his lunch."

At that revelation, Ellen let out a laugh. "Typical of the sly old fox killing two birds with one stone."

By this time they had reached the garage, Brent flashed another of his smiles. "Thank you for this. I had a wonderful time I'd like to see you again."

Ellen leant over "I'd like that very much." The kiss that followed was very enjoyable too.

A short time later Ellen once more pulled into the Town Hall parking lot. The sight of an ambulance parked outside the hall was a cause for worry. The short look she got at the driver quickly changed worry to fear as she thought she recognized the man. It was her old playmate Adolph, the one that got away. He had shaved off the little toothbrush moustache that had caused the Domino Lady give him the nickname Adolph but she recognized the cruel features.

He must have escaped and took refuge with more Bund sympathizers. This must be their back up plan, Ellen reasoned as she pulled into the parking spot. She had noticed a Ladies' Room as she left earlier and it was there she headed with her handbag. Once again the blonde bombshell found herself in her lingerie racing to become the Domino Lady to rescue a friend. Ellen slipped on her special white dress with a daring décolletage and a black cape to cover her shoulders. She added the Domino mask that concealed her identity, checking her appearance in the mirror.

Since the previous night, there had been no opportunity to make more of her special knockout formula. Her only dose was in the special trick flower she pinned on the dress' halter neck to complete her ensemble. She still had the sap and her trusty little automatic. Just like the early days of the Domino Lady.

Domino Lady prowled the hallways making her way to the Mayor's office. This was a race against time, Ellen rarely appeared as the Domino Lady in daylight hours and Brent was due back at any moment. In spite of her mask, the secretary would be almost certain to recognize her.

Even though she was risking everything, Domino Lady was calm and precise. Like a black and white spectre, Domino Lady silently swept through the Town Hall towards her uncle's office.

She peered around the doorframe and saw a white uniformed ambulance attendant injecting the sleeping Dave Thornby with what she hoped was a knockout drug. The old man was certainly going to have a good rest today. Ellen hoped that the drug wasn't addictive given the amount that had been given to the old man over the past two days.

The first ambulance attendant signaled to a second standing beside a stretcher. Together they grabbed the old man's arms and legs and hoisted him towards the stretcher. Suddenly, the man holding Thornby's arms lost his grip and the unconscious man's back and skull made a rather hard landing on the floor. Even with the layer of carpet muffling the sound, there was a loud thump.

"Dumbkomf!" cursed the second attendant.

The Domino Lady had seen and heard enough to be sure that she had not been mistaken with her identification of Adolph earlier. There was second abduction attempt taking place.

The young avenger burst into the room and made for the man bending down to pick up her uncle. Ellen activated the flower pinned to the halter neck of her dress and a spray of her own special knockout formula sprayed in his face. The gas had no side effects and was not addictive. It was also fast acting and burly ambulance attendant toppled over, his unconscious body sprawled over his victim.

Like a dervish, Domino Lady spun to face the second man. For a second, the pair sized each other up. Domino Lady had the sap in her hand and her gun was in its holster. Through much practice, Domino Lady was able to draw and shoot within a half second.

The Bundist stood over a foot taller than Ellen and was nearly double the weight. The man appeared to be made of muscle. His bullet head was nearly bald with lumps of gristle for nose and ears, suggesting that he made his living through the pugilistic arts. Ellen had his name on the tip of her tongue but couldn't quite recall it.

"Nein!" the big man roared and swung his sledgehammer like fists.

Domino Lady threw the blackjack and it flew true smashing the nose gristle. There was a loud snap and blood began to pour from the nostrils. The big man merely smiled, blood staining his teeth.

"Fraulein, I have been hit by Dempsey, your love tap is nothing. "

It was then that Ellen recalled when and where she recognized the boxer from. Her father had taken her to a small travelling boxing show before she left for Berkeley. The main attraction was "Harry the Hun," the show offered a hundred dollars to anyone who could last two full rounds with him. No-one that day had claimed the money and he taunted the crowd in the same fashion.

The challengers that day had been bound by the rules of boxing, Domino Lady was not. She ducked under a wild haymaker and kicked the side of her shoe into the boxer's shin just below the knee and stomped down, dragging along the shin bone until her foot struck the top of his foot. The lithe vigilante then danced away.

Harry the Hun grunted in surprise at the unorthodox move. Unlike his nose, that had been broken so many times he could reset it himself, his legs had rarely been attacked this pain was both new and unpleasant. The nerve endings in his shins were loudly sending a message of pain. The big man raised his leg and rubbed the injured limb.

The Domino Lady reached into her décolletage and pulled her trusty hand gun. For a moment she considered killing this man mountain, but Domino Lady was no killer. She had never taken a life in her crime fighting career and she was not about to start now.

As the German boxer hopped around the room, he turned his back on the masked vigilante. Ellen whipped the pistol into his back just over the liver. Instantly the big man toppled over, the excruciating pain so much that he passed out. Domino Lady had once seen a boxing match where the fight had ended from such a blow and the boxer had curled up in the fetal position and Ellen hoped for a similar reaction in this case. Harry's passing out showed that her blow was even more successful than she had hoped.

Domino Lady went behind the desk and picked up the phone. She had memorized the number that Detective Faraday had given her the night before. The call went right through to the detective's desk.

"This is the Domino Lady. The Bund has made another attempt to kidnap Mayor Thornby, two of the kidnappers are in his office at City Hall. The third is outside by the ambulance they planned to use as a getaway vehicle, pretending that the Mayor was ill."

Before the detective could ask any more questions, Domino Lady hung up the phone. Her voice had been all business, unlike the demure and slightly flirtatious tone that she had used the night before talking with the detective. Hopefully, that and the short message was enough that Faraday wouldn't be able to identify Ellen Patrick as the Domino Lady.

But Domino Lady had far more pressing concerns, not only would the police be in their way but so was Ellen's lunch date Brent Richards and he was certain to recognize Ellen Patrick under the mask of the Domino Lady. The daring young adventuress wanted to capture the vicious Bundist she had nicknamed Adolph. He had eluded capture once and immediately threatened her family again. Ellen meant to capture the Bundist even if it came at the cost of exposing herself as the Domino Lady.

As she ran through the halls, Ellen realized that she been playing with fire with her secret identity. During the Black Legion affair, Paul Cathern had penetrated her disguise and knew that Ellen was the Domino Lady. Luckily, after saving his life he was keeping her secret. But there was no guarantee that if someone else were to uncover her secret they would also keep it.

But none of that mattered. If it meant saving another life or ending the California political machine that killed her father Ellen Patrick would gladly give up her secret life as the Domino Lady but until then she would continue her crime fighting activities. The Domino Lady would be fighting crime as long as she was able.

She made it to the front door. The ambulance was still there. That meant that Adolph hadn't gotten spooked waiting for his henchmen.

The Bundist was leaning on the vehicle. Ellen noticed that he had shaved off the moustache but the strong California sun had tanned the rest of his face leaving a white patch of skin above his upper lip. More than one married man had been caught out by the band of pale skin on their ring finger, trying to talk Ellen Patrick into bed. Adolph might as well kept his moustache, the patch of lily white skin probably drew more attention to him.

Adolph appeared nonchalant but as Domino Lady watched she could see that the little man's eyes were always in motion. The man stretched and the afternoon sun caught the blade of his knife. The glint of light confirmed that Bundist was armed.

Time was running out for the Domino Lady. She had to move quickly, once Adolph heard the police sirens he was sure to flee. She briefly considered shooting out the tires but the gunshot was likely to cause a panic. In the circumstances Adolph was unlikely to be distracted by the sight of a shapely leg in fine silk stockings; it was a trick the Domino Lady had used on more than one occasion.

It was a desperate move, but last time she was in New York staying at the Waldorf-Anthony she had been introduced to Kent. The strange and shadowy man was widely travelled and mentioned that while serving in the court of the Czar, he had seen a magician Kosmo perform amazing feats with his cape. Ellen hadn't believed the man until later, he used a Baritsu move with his cloak to save the life of the Domino Lady.

Ellen had never been able to master the move but it seemed the only way to capture Adolph without drawing attention. Domino Lady removed her cape, baring her shoulders and walked out the door.

Adolph saw the door open and any trace of his nonchalance was gone and a nasty grin curled the corners of his mouth. The grin was soon replaced by a snarl as he saw the Domino Lady.

"You!" he snarled as he recognized the blonde avenger. He brought his knife up to attack the woman who had already humiliated him.

Domino Lady snapped her wrist and the cape flowed across to Adolph. The corner of the cape wrapped around his wrist and snapped on a nerve. Immediately Adolph released his grip on the blade. The clatter of the knife hitting the ground was drowned out but the yell of surprise from the Bundist.

Domino Lady pulled on her cape with her right hand and let loose with a left cross. Adolph spun around causing the cape to come loose.

Just then the sound of a police siren cut through the air. Adolph then fumbled in his pockets for the keys. In his haste the keys slipped from his fingers. The Bundist let loose with a German curse word that the Domino Lady had only heard once before, her companion in Berlin refused to tell her what it meant given that it was so vulgar.

If looks could kill, Domino Lady's life would have been finished then and there so full of hatred and malice was the glare the German sympathizer locked onto her before he decided that discretion was the better part of valor and fled on foot.

Domino Lady briefly considered following the man but the siren was getting louder and the immediate threat was over. This time, at least, the police were aware that one of the conspirators had escaped and would be on the alert. Ellen retreated back into the Town Hall and returned to the restrooms where she had changed a few minutes earlier. Her change back to Ellen Patrick was nearly as fast as the one to the Domino Lady. Ellen then returned to her car and she opened the boot and pulled out something she had bought earlier in the day and would help to explain the delay if her lunch companion returned. Speak of the devil, thought Ellen as she saw Brent drive into the car park.

"Sorry, I took so long. I had to dispute the price they tried charge me." The young politician announced as he got out of the car.

"I just got here myself," Ellen said, lifting out a hatbox from the trunk of her car, "I remembered a lovely haberdasher and I just had to visit."

The young man just barely restrained the glazed look the Ellen found that most men adopted at the mention of shopping. After establishing her alibi, Ellen changed the subject. "Did you see the ambulance on the way in? I hope nothing has happened to Uncle Dave."

"I'm sure the old man is alright. He's a tough old bird. We occasionally get ambulance crews drop by for a cup of coffee, I'm sure it's nothing." Brent told Ellen. But the worried tone in his voice gave lie to his words. "Let's go show him your new hat."

Ellen and Brent then walked into the rear entrance of the town hall. The police sirens were coming closer and the worried look on Brent's face only intensified. Ellen was sure that her own face was starting to look more worried.

By chance, the police arrived at the Mayor's office at the same time as Ellen and Brent arrived. Brent immediately introduced himself and Ellen to the two uniformed officers as they were about to open the door. The older of the two officers introduced himself as Sergeant Garcia and apprised the secretary of the Domino Lady's call to the police of another kidnapping attempt.

Ellen made the expected feminine noises that a concerned family member was expected to make at such news. The Sergeant stroked his long moustaches "Miss Ellen," he boomed, "I'm convinced this is just some college prank. A couple of the boys probably took an ambulance, tried to stir up some trouble and got one of their girlfriend's to call as the Domino Lady."

The swarthy officer let loose with a belly laugh. "I mean everyone knows there's no Domino Lady, she's just some Hollywood publicity stunt."

The laughter was soon silenced as the office door was opened and three unconscious bodies greeted the eyes of the four investigators. The black cards on the white uniforms of the two kidnappers stood out like the proverbial sore thumb. The younger officer, Patrolman Hawke picked up one of the cards and let loose with a low whistle. "Compliments of The Domino Lady." He read to the group.

Ellen stole a glance at Sergeant Gonzales during the reading. His face was going a rather interesting shade of red; Ellen couldn't tell if it was from embarrassment or anger.

At that moment Harry the Hun elected to wake up. Hawke lived up to his namesake flying across the room after the big German hit him.

Although surprised, the large Sargeant was quick to react with his pistol. A crimson flower of blood appeared in the middle of Harry's forehead as the bullet burrowed into his brain.

Ellen ran to the fallen officer. He was shaken and appeared to have no broken bones. Officer Hawke was lucky that the Hun was groggy otherwise he may have been more seriously injured. Although Ellen suspected the man might not feel so lucky the next day when he woke up stiff and bruised.

Both police officers were somewhat more cautious approaching the other faux ambulance officer. But there was no need to worry; the Domino Lady's gas would keep him unconscious for at least another forty minutes. But neither officer knew that and Ellen was in no position to advise them otherwise.

With Harry the Hun pushing up daisies and his unconscious confederate safely in handcuffs, the police officers were able to turn their attentions to the mayor. Ellen was immediately at his side as soon as the police officers advised her it was safe.

She stayed with him as Garcia called for an ambulance and to report to headquarters. There was no embarrassment in the burly police officer's voice as he advised that they had captured one of the kidnappers. Within ten minutes the mayor's office was full of ambulance and police officers.

Ellen noticed Detectives Butler and Faraday talking with Garcia as she followed Dave's stretcher through the crowd. Constable Hawke winced as he waved before being scolded by the ambulance officer examining him. In the wake of the mayor, another ambulance crew brought through the unconscious Bundist handcuffed to the stretcher.

Ellen drove back to the house to pick up her Aunt Mary. The police had already called her and Ellen found the older woman waiting on the porch.

As soon as Mary was in the passenger seat she launched into a tirade about her stubborn mule-headed husband. Ellen just listened knowing her aunt was worried and was just venting some of tension. Mary may have threatened to throttle her husband on the way there but as soon as she got to his bedside and found him awake the older woman hugged him and near smothered him with kisses.

After a few minutes, Dave Thornby stopped his wife. "Takes more than a couple of Huns to take me out, why I remember back in the Great War knocking out more than a couple of Kraut lovers …"

"That was twenty years ago." Interrupted Mary. "And the doctor told you not to get excited."

Ellen had never seen her aunt so forceful with her uncle; two attacks in as many days would be enough to scare anyone. Of course, putting the scare into men like Owen Patrick and Dave Thornby was most likely to result in a fierce determination to do the very thing you were trying to prevent them from doing. Ellen knew that nothing short of death would stop her uncle from opening the bridge and she had her doubts if the Grim Reaper himself would be effective.

The beautiful socialite had reason to revisit that thought a few days later as the image of her defiant uncle sat above the headline, "MAYOR REFUSES TO BUDGE OVER BRIDGE" on the front page of The Daily Sentinel. After an overnight stay, Dave had been released and even taken a couple of days away from the office, but nothing was going to stop the opening of his bridge.

Ellen had been on alert but as there had been no new attacks she had spent the last two evenings out on the town. Detective Faraday had taken her dancing the night before last, the detective had showered her with champagne and told her that he was looking on moving on from Berkley Police, applying for jobs with the Neptune and Palm City departments. Ellen knew the signs of a man setting himself up to make a proposal to her but the socialite was an expert at deflecting proposals and the pair parted as friends.

The previous evening had been spent dining with Brent Richards followed by a movie. The conversation was stimulating and reminded Ellen of her childhood, sitting on the stairs and listening to the after dinner conversations of her parents and their guests. Brent was extremely well informed on a number of topics and the pair had a lively discussion on the architectural style of California including the recent work of Frank Lloyd Wright.

While the dates were for pleasure, Faraday kept her up to date with the police investigation and the search for Adolph. The captured Bundists

As soon as Mary was in the passenger seat she launched into a tirade...

hadn't spoken to the police. Richards during his date kept her informed on the city hall gossip and the preparations for the bridge opening.

The daring young adventuress was hoping that Adolph had given up on trying to kidnap her uncle or otherwise disrupt the bridge opening but something told her that the Bundist was merely biding his time until the bridge dedication.

Much to the disappointment of her two beaus, Ellen passed on their company on the night before the big ceremony. While she told both men that she was meeting an old friend from her student days, but the truth was it was not Ellen Patrick going out for a night on the town but another nocturnal adventure for the Domino Lady.

An afternoon visit to her old chemistry professor at Berkeley had given her the opportunity to replenish her knockout formula. Early in her crusade, Ellen had decided that she would not be a killer, one day the Domino Lady may take another's life but so far she had avoided that. The knockout formula was a large part of how she had avoided killing for so long. The memory of when she thought she had killed. J. Thomas Saint, the crooked District Attorney working for the Black Legion was enough to make her glad she had a good supply of the drug.

Domino Lady stood in a small thicket of trees looking over the ornamental lake in the middle of the park. The wooden bridge had been freshly painted in red and white. In the darkness it looked black and white matching Domino Lady's own color scheme. A cool breeze blew over the lake, enough to tousle Domino Lady's luxurious blonde locks and bring goose bumps to her bare shoulders. The Domino Lady pulled her black cape around herself to warm herself and further blend into the shadows.

After a couple of hours the voluptuous vigilante was starting to think that this stakeout was just a wild goose chase. She could feel the midnight dark pressing in on her. Her eyelids were starting to droop and the Domino Lady was ready to hit the sheets. Just as she was about to prepare to leave, a blob of darkness moved near the bridge. All traces of fatigue left her body as she pulled her gun. Domino Lady moved across the park. Her black cape shielded most of her from view, only someone directly in front would have noticed her white dress.

Her little gun led the way as she moved closer to the bridge. Her keen brown eyes scanned the landscape seeking out the source of the movement or any other threats. The movement was not repeated. Domino Lady started doubting if she had seen anything.

As she reached the bridge, Ellen reached into her bag and pulled out a pencil flashlight. The tiny light source illuminated the edge of the bridge.

"Who's out there? Is it a haint?" came a gravelly voice tinged with fear, from under the bridge, causing the Domino Lady to conjure visions of an ogre.

"Come out where I can see you." Called the curvaceous crime-fighter to the ogre under the bridge.

"I'm coming" grumbled the voice. A tramp in a rumpled suit crawled out from under the bridge carrying his bindle. "You don't sound like any dick, I've met before."

The torch illuminated the curly haired man. "I was just looking for a place to flop for the night." He explained.

"The bridge isn't a good place to flop for the night or did the Bund send you?" interrogated the Domino Lady.

"I'm no Kraut lover." Snapped the hobo, shielding his eyes from the light. "Lord knows I killed enough of them in the war, but I've had enough of that. I'll find another spot to flop."

With that the tramp slung his bindle over his shoulder and walked off. Domino Lady flicked on the safety of her gun and released the breath she had been holding. After a few minutes, the surge of adrenaline began to wash away and the fatigue began to set in again. Ellen's instinct was that nothing else was going to happen tonight, if anything was going to happen it would be during the ceremony.

The next morning found the socialite yawning over her coffee. Dave took the opportunity to tease his niece.

"You young ones, no stamina. Why when I was in college...."

"You worked six jobs, played football, lacrosse and baseball, went to dances and still had time to study and pass summa cum laude without any sleep or yawning." Ellen finished. "You might have given me this speech when I was at Berkeley."

"It was only two jobs." Dave replied with a big grin. "And I'm sure I only said it once or twice."

After the hearty breakfast Mary had cooked, everyone got ready for the dedication ceremony. Ellen offered to drive, if there was any trouble from the Bund, the Domino Lady's crime fighting ensemble was in the trunk ready for action.

The park had been decorated with Union Jacks and Old Glory signifying Anglo-American unity. The bridge opening was a celebration and families had come to the park for the event. Food vendors walked the park hawking their wares.

As she drove down the road, Ellen's keen brown eyes scanned the crowds searching for the threat she was certain to be there. The large event had brought out the newspaper reporters and her uncle had confided that a cameraman from the newsreels would be there. Any disturbance would be sure to be spread far and wide. Ellen recalled the opening of the Sydney Harbor Bridge a few years back, a man on horseback had charged out of the crowd and cut the ribbon before the official ceremony. Ellen had seen to footage in newsreel a few weeks later, a similar embarrassment here might make it halfway around the world too and could cause serious harm to any run for Governor her uncle was to make. California politics needed more men like Dave Thornby if there was any hope to topple the corrupt political machine that had killed her father.

The party drove past a black truck, Ellen thought for a second that it may have been the one used in the first kidnapping attempt but it was impossible to tell as there were any number of black trucks driving around. Ellen mentally berated herself; she was jumping at shadows and leaping to conclusions. If she kept this up she'd be too tired to do anything if there was another attempt to kidnap her uncle.

A small smile rose on her cupid bow lips as Ellen eased the car into the space reserved for her uncle and soon the party was on their way to the bridge. Dave carried the picnic basket that his wife had prepared the night before. Ellen was still on alert scanning the crowd. She'd spotted Butler and Faraday patrolling the crowd and Brent was standing by the podium. Then it happened as she looked around out of corner of her eye she caught a glimpse of another familiar face, a rather unwelcome one at that. It was her old friend Adolph. Her instincts were right.

Ellen made a hasty excuse to her aunt and uncle that she had forgotten something in the car and followed the wily Bundist through the crowd. Adolph had attacked her family twice now and avoided justice both times, the Domino Lady was determined that this third attempt would be his last.

The beautiful blonde moved through the crowd following her prey. She felt several sets of eyes following her through the crowd but Ellen knew that it was the type of admiring look that a stunningly gorgeous woman like herself usually got. She even heard a few wives berating their husbands for staring. As the Domino Lady, Ellen had developed a sensitivity to a malicious gaze, it had saved her life on more than one occasion, and there was nothing like that in the crowd.

Ellen could see the black truck, the one she had dismissed earlier up ahead; it appeared to be Adolph's destination. Thankfully they had to pass nearby the roadster and if she moved quickly, Ellen would be able to change into the Domino Lady and intercept the truck.

Ellen was grateful that her aunt had insisted that she put up the canvas roof before they left, it was a little cramped but it offered enough privacy for Ellen to peel off the floral sundress. Had anyone looked they would have seen the beautiful blonde in her undergarments, but with the ease of much practice Ellen had soon donned the slinky white dress that hugged her delectable curves. The low cut halter neck offered a tantalizing hint of the swell of her ductile lunettes and had befuddled and distracted more than one criminal making him putty in the hands of the Domino Lady. Ellen pulled on the black cape that covered her shoulders. The outfit was completed by the black domino mask that framed her brown eyes. The Domino Lady accessorized with her trusty gun and her special handbag. Ellen was about to don her special knockout flower but remembered Coco Chanel's advice and decided against it. The Domino Lady was ready for action.

With the speed and grace of a cheetah, Domino Lady raced to her target. She could see Adolph through the windscreen of the truck. The Bundist was looking dirty and unkempt, a three day growth covered his face but there was no mistaking the fanatical fire in his eyes. Domino Lady was still twenty feet away when their eyes met. She could see Adolph's eyes widen in surprise and his lips form a particularly vile German phrase.

The rumble of the truck engine shattered the tranquil sounds of children playing and laughter of picnicking families. To the Domino Lady's analytical mind it signaled the desperate Bundist's plan. That maniac was going to plough the truck through the crowd and into the bridge, all to make a statement about foreign policy.

The truck lurched out of the parking bay and instead of heading right towards the bridge; it turned left and headed straight at the vivacious vigilante. Adolph was looking to either eliminate the threat that had foiled his last two attempts at stopping the bridge opening or settling a personal score, either way the effect was the same, a very large black truck was going to run over the Domino Lady unless she acted quickly.

Domino Lady stopped in her tracks and calmly brought up her pistol. The epitome of grace under pressure Domino Lady took her time and located her target. Her finger squeezed the trigger and fired the weapon. The bullet flew true and shattered the windscreen. In a vain attempt to avoid the shot, Adolph had yanked the wheel into a sharp right turn.

The shattered windscreen did not have the desired effect; Adolph did not stop the truck. The pistol was already aligning itself on the next target, the front left tire. Reluctantly, Domino Lady pulled the trigger, it was the only target on the truck that would be affected enough by her bullets that it might disable the truck. The boom of the pistol was soon followed by the pop of the tire. It may have been Ellen's imagination but she swore she heard the air rush through the rupture. To Ellen's dismay the sudden deflation coupled with the sharp turn was enough to destabilize the truck and it soon started to topple. The truck rolled to the left, away from the crowd of people.

Domino Lady made a tactical retreat away from the path of the rolling truck but raced towards the wreck to see if there was anything she could do for the driver. The truck's cabin had been the first thing to hit the ground and crumpled like tissue paper crushing the driver into a bloody pulp. One glance was enough to see that Adolph was beyond the help of any medical attention. The triple threat of the Bund was now over. She considered leaving one of her calling cards, but it seemed too ghoulish to claim credit for this and it would be better for this to be thought of as an accident.

Domino Lady was aware that the crash would soon bring a curious crowd and she disappeared. After a quick change into her sundress Ellen Patrick joined the crowd of onlookers. She spotted Detective Butler, the burly Irishman stood at the front of the crowd trying to keep the sight of the mangled man from the delicate eyes of the women and children. Several men from the crowd were at the crush truck trying vainly to free the corpse.

Ellen felt a tap on her shoulder, and a familiar deep voice whisper in her ear. "Careful miss, a delicate young thing like yourself shouldn't see things like this."

Detective Faraday's voice sent shivers along her spine, and in trembling voice Ellen asked what had happened. The young detective said that the driver appeared to have a fit and lost control of the truck, before a burst tire sent it into a roll. Faraday then suggested that Ellen would be better with her aunt and uncle down at the stage. The blonde nodded her agreement and moved away from the accident scene.

Ellen's heart soared at the realization that the Bundist threat to her uncle was finally over. Even better was the fact that the official story while close enough to the facts, left out the involvement of the Domino Lady in the events. It was not her intent to kill Adolph but his actions had led to his own demise. The Domino Lady's position was not to take human life.

Her shot into the windscreen had been a warning and the tire shot was to disable the truck. The Domino Lady was not a murderer.

As she reached the stage, Mary came down and embraced her niece. "We were so worried when we heard the crash, thank God you are alright."

"I'm alright, some poor truck driver lost control of his truck." Ellen advised.

In light of the tragedy, Dave Thornby took to the stage and announced that the opening was postponed until the next day out of respect to the deceased trucker and to allow the wreck to be towed away and the park cleaned.

The next day saw Ellen and the Thornbys return to Holmes Park to an even larger crowd than the day before. The media attention of the crash the day before had resulted in a great deal of inadvertent publicity for the bridge dedication. Ellen looked around the crowd and saw a larger contingent of police than the day before. She took the time to say greet Patrolman Hawke, he advised that his encounter with Harry the Hun had only resulted in a few bruises and no serious injuries. Ellen was pleased to hear that the young officer had no lasting injuries. The young patrolman shared that the truck crash the day before had been declared an accident with no suspicious circumstances.

Ellen exchanged a few more pleasantries with the young officer. He was star struck by the tales of Hollywood Ellen told him. Hawke then thrilled her with stories about his aviator brother. The conversation only ended with the start of the ceremony.

Ellen made her way to the stage and took her seat beside her Uncle and Aunt. Brent opened the ceremony and called for a moment of silence for the driver who had lost his life the day before. He then introduced the Mayor. After the applause died down, the older man came to the lectern and started his speech.

"When I was in college here in Berkeley, I met a young man Owen Patrick. After we graduated we decided to travel the Continent. While we were in England, The Great War was declared. Being young and stupid we joined the British Army. As a proud Irishman, there was no other choice for Owen Patrick. The things we saw in the trenches, gave us a maturity and insight that we may never gained otherwise. It made us realize that we should enter politics when we get home and try to build a better world."

Dave paused for a moment and took a sip of water. "And that's what we did. Owen Patrick worked tirelessly to build a better world. Sadly, he found that not everyone appreciated that and three years ago he was murdered. So he cannot be here to see this bridge. This bridge that symbolizes the friendship between America and Great Britain that symbolizes the hope that Owen and I had for the future. A future where justice and right will prevail. A future where his daughter Ellen will grow up and raise children of her own."

Dave indicated Ellen sitting on the stage. "I have achieved all I can as your mayor, to make our vision for the future a reality I wish to announce that I will be running for The Governor of California."

At this news the crowd erupted into applause. When the noise abated, Dave called Brent back to the microphone. The young man looked slightly nervous standing beside his mentor. Dave continued. "I give to you my running mate, the future Lieutenant Governor Brent Richards."

The newsmen in the crowd started yell questions. The news reel cameraman furiously turned the handles of their machines, capturing the announcement and the reaction to play in cinemas across the state and possibly the country.

With the bridge open and the threat to her Uncle over, Ellen knew that it was time to head for home. For the first time since the death of her father, she hopeful for the future. With good men like Dave Thornby and Brent Richards in office, backed by honest police like Butler, Faraday and Hawke, it may no longer be necessary for her to don a domino mask to achieve justice. In any case, after this triple threat she'd earned a couple of days off.

After the long drive home, she ran a hot soothing bubble bath and poured a glass of champagne. Ellen peeled off the travel soiled clothes and eased her tired and weary body into the bubbles. The heat of the water soaked into her shapely body as she sipped the champers, after all a girl needed to pamper herself sometimes.

The End

THE DOMINO LADY WRITTEN

I remember heading to the comic shop and finding The Complete Adventures of the Domino Lady. The cover by James Steranko showed The Domino Lady stepping out of the shadows ready for adventure. That's how I met The Domino Lady. I devoured the six pulp adventures by Lars Anderson and the new adventure by Steranko himself. Over the years, I found several continuations by other authors, including some of the Eros Comix books.

The Domino Lady became an influence on my writing. My characters, The Silhouette and Risqué, owe a debt to The Domino Lady. So when I heard that Airship 27 was doing Domino Lady Anthologies I was keen to contribute.

In my research for another story, I read about the opening of the Sydney Harbour Bridge. Several threats were made against Premier Jack Lang at the time, nothing came of the threats and Lang opened the bridge after a minor disturbance. The New Guard was a group of World War One veterans who were loyal to the British Empire and felt that Lang opening the bridge was disrespectful to the King. They threated to kidnap Lang to prevent him from opening the bridge, one plot was running Lang off the road, another involved faking an illness and whisking Lang off in an ambulance. In reality, these plots were just bluster from Eric Campbell, the leader of the New Guard. In the end his second in command Captain Philip De Groot, rode onto the bridge and cut the ribbon with sabre declaring the bridge open for "all decent and respectable people of New South Wales." The bridge opening was recorded by the newsreel cameras and Lang's embarrassment was shown around the world, reportedly King George V laughed at the footage. The New Guard lost most of its relevance after Lang was dismissed later that year and became more of a fascist organisation.

I wondered if there was another reason that none of the New Guard's threats came to fruition and that became the start of this story. The bridge opened in 1932 making it too early for The Domino Lady but Ellen Patrick would have known a great many people from her father's political career, one of which would have been responsible for a similar public work that would have an opening ceremony and raised the ire of a group such as the American German Bund.

I reread the original stories by Lars Anderson, (a hardship, I know) there was no one suitable from those stories, so I invented Dave and Mary Thornby, old friends of Ellen Patrick's parents. Lars Anderson didn't have any older characters as all of Ellen's friends all came from her time at Berkeley so this was something I could rectify. Making Dave Thornby a surrogate father figure, Ellen had an added incentive to save him given that she wasn't able to save her father.

Each of the original stories had a love interest for Ellen Patrick and I decided to up the ante and give her one for each threat. If you have read the story, you'll recall that there was only two romantic interests, try as I might I couldn't find a way to introduce a third man in Ellen's life especially as both her romantic rivals were to be at the third threat.

One of the things about Lars Anderson that I wanted to use were his descriptions of Ellen Patrick and her physical charms. Kissable shoulders, ductile lunettes and butter colored hair with several quick changes of clothing to showcase them all. In my first draft I went overboard with the kissable shoulders, one of my beta readers declared after a few paragraphs that they got it, her shoulders were kissable. I had to work a bit harder to get the ductile lunettes into the story.

BRAD MENGEL— works in Australia's criminal justice system. Before that he was trolley boy, a barman, an office manager and a teacher. A lifelong reader and pulp fan it was natural that he would turn to writing.

His book Serial *Vigilantes of Paperback Fiction: An Encyclopedia from Able Team to Z-Comm* (McFarland, 2009) was the first book to examine vigilante fiction of the 70s and 80s. He has also contributed stories to *Tales of The Shadowmen* #3 & #7, *Pro Se Presents* Nov 2012, *Charles Boeckman Presents Johnny Nickle, Pulp Obscura: Senorita Scorpion* and *Blood & Tacos* #4 and *The Destroyer: More Blood*. His series *Australis Incognito* is coming soon from Pro Se.

THE MURDER GAMES
Robert M. Ricci

Los Angeles - 1936

The glare of the flashbulbs blinded Ellen Patrick. Instinctively, she crouched into a combat pose before remembering her location. Flushed with embarrassment, she rallied to save face.

"Are you ready for the Olympics? I am!"

The crowd roared with approval.

The ballroom of the Hollywood Roosevelt was filled to capacity with some of the country's finest socialites, a tribute to Ellen's influence, as she was solely responsible for the unofficial fundraiser.

Many Americans were divided regarding the German Olympics. The Jewish population sought a boycott of the event, while athletes begged not to be cheated out of an opportunity to smear dirt in Hitler's face. As a highly regarded former athlete, Ellen personally knew many of the competitors, as well as their foreign rivals, and she had decided to support their cause to compete.

Thus, here she was, tonight, hosting an unsanctioned event at one of the premiere hotels on the west coast.

Ellen raised her hand for the crowd to halt their applause as she read from a hastily prepared speech.

"Ladies and gentlemen, thank you for coming tonight. I'm sure all of you remember the wonderful games our very own Los Angeles put on four years ago, I certainly do. My father took me to see that spectacle, and it's a memory I'll cherish the rest of my life." She raised her champagne glass and lifted her eyes to the heavens. "Thank you, Daddy."

Once again the crowd erupted in a polite round of applause, remembering Owen Patrick, the beloved District Attorney who had been slain by underworld thugs.

"My father was immensely proud of that event and what it represented around the world and that is why I honor his memory in hosting this reception tonight in hopes that we can put aside the political differences this evening and rejoice in the common bond that draws these athletes from all around the globe."

She glanced over at one of the lighting technicians who on cue placed a spotlight on a gentleman at the right of the stage. He was a tall, imposing figure dressed in formal wear. The shine of the harsh light reflected on his bald head, giving his posture an even more majestic stance.

"I draw your attention to our distinguished guest, straight from the German heartland, Doctor Franz Hinnenburg, ambassador to the games who graciously honors us with his presence tonight."

The crowd responded sluggishly with a polite splatter of light hand-claps.

Ellen cleared her throat nervously as the light swiftly revolved back toward her. Many Americans were angered by Hitler's bravado and claims of superiority. The backlash inevitably fell upon all Germans.

"Please welcome Doctor Hinnenburg to our fine city and enjoy your evening." She raised her glass again. "Don't forget to open those checkbooks. Our young athletes need your support when they head over to Berlin to bring back the gold!"

Ellen's enthusiasm was contagious. The usually contrite highbrow folks in the room exploded with the excitement that only a major sporting event could promise. She exited the stage, splendid in her dark evening gown.

Doctor Franz Hinnenburg greeted her at the last stair.

"Thank you for that kind introduction."

Ellen nodded, her eyes taking in the man's sculpted physique. "My pleasure, Doctor. You look like you could challenge some of these young athletes tonight."

Hinnenburg beamed his approval. "It is true. At one time I was a force to be reckoned with until I shattered my ankle serving in the military. Sadly, my days of physical prowess are in the past, I am now purely a man of science."

Ellen smiled coyly. "I'm sure you can still muster up the energy when necessary."

The burly German snickered. "I like you, Ellen Patrick. " He reached out and touched a strand of her hair. "Forgive my boldness; your beauty and stature have me thinking that you, too, could be competing in these games. In fact, my researchers told me that while at Berkeley you were actually a front runner for the American team?"

"True," Ellen replied. "But sadly I injured myself right before the trials and had to withdraw."

Hinnenburg frowned. "A pity... I'm sure you would have fared well."

"Thank you, but I find it detrimental to dwell on what might have been. I live for the here and now."

Ellen enjoyed flirting with the big German doctor. She felt no need to tell him the truth regarding her Olympic withdrawal. She had feigned her injury, unable to commit the time and effort necessary to compete in the games. She instead applied that energy and intensity into her other passion.

Ellen Patrick's life was shattered the day her father was assassinated. Olympic dreams were cast aside as Ellen concentrated her unique intensity on a new endeavor. She had vowed to bring her father's killers to justice and to wipeout all criminal element that preyed on good, hardworking people of her city.

In that moment, the sentinel of liberty, Domino Lady was born.

Hinnenburg interrupted her reflection. "Someone so young, yet so powerful..." He swept an arm toward the crowd. "You command an audience."

Ellen feigned modesty. "Some of these folks remember my father, others are just failed jocks living the fantasy through these young kids, and some of them are just here for exposure to the press. I'm just a portal to make it happen."

Hinnenburg grabbed two fresh glasses of champagne from a waiter who was passing by. "No, my friend, you are more than meets the eye." He smiled warmly at her.

Ellen felt herself being drawn to the man. "Enough about me, tell me about these games. You have a hard act to follow with the wonderful show America put on four years ago."

"True, yes but since that time our homeland has weeded out its inferiors and through a carefully constructed master plan we have created a race of Aryan Supermen who will dominate these games on a level never before imagined."

Ellen raised an eyebrow. "Supermen? And what of your female athletes? They don't deserve the same 'master plan'?"

Hinnenburg coughed nervously. "You misunderstood my words."

"Did I?" Ellen countered.

"The medical and scientific breakthroughs we Germans have achieved will be showcased for the world at these summer games before we share the results with the rest of the world."

Ellen Patrick felt a shiver go down her spine. "Just how will these results be shared, Doctor? On the playing field or perhaps someday on the battlefield?"

Hinnenburg laughed nervously, before regaining his composure and wrapping an arm around Ellen's shoulder. His fingers on her bare skin caused her to tingle.

"I am a man of science, Ellen Patrick. As such I am dedicated to advance the cause of mankind; all mankind."

Ellen smiled, her mood swaying back in the doctor's favor. His arrogance was childish but charming. "I think our boys and girls will prove you wrong, Doctor."

"I admire the spunk of your youthful hope, but I disagree immensely. Forgive me but your country's athletic pool has no cohesiveness. It's too diverse. You have teams made up of different races and backgrounds. They can't possibly mesh together the way our German athletes do. Victory is assured. It will be the greatest domination in Olympic history."

"You seem convinced."

He nodded. "I am sure of it." He grabbed her hand and kissed it. "The women of Germany are fortunate indeed that you are not competing. With your magnificent body and golden locks, I fear the medals might have had a chance to flee our motherland. If I didn't know better I would swear you were a member of the dominant race."

"Forgive my rudeness, Doctor Hinnenburg, but I need some fresh air. Your blustery bragging has filled this ballroom with enough hot air to float one of your zeppelins halfway around the globe."

She winked at him, before shimmying toward the center of a small crowd that had gathered. Franz Hinnenburg stared defiantly at her departing figure before glancing at his German timepiece. It read nine o'clock. The true 'master' plan was about to go into action.

Knock! Knock!

The sound of rapping on the door woke Ellen Patrick from her slumber. Reflexively, she bolted out of bed. She caught a glimpse of her evening gown folded over the corner chair and remembered she was naked.

"Hold your horses!" she demanded.

She quickly grabbed a satin night robe from the closet and donned it. She tied the sash around her waist and peered through the keyhole. On the other side of the doorway she spotted the familiar uniform of Jimmy the porter.

The dark skinned youth bared his pearly whites and announced himself.

"It's just me, Jimmy, Miss Patrick." He quickly doffed his bell cap. "I done brought your morning paper like you requested."

Ellen unlocked the door and opened it.

"Jimmy, I told you to address me as Ellen."

"Course Miss Ellen."

The bubbly porter was careful to keep his eyes cast down in respect, but this caused his eyes to focus down on Ellen's legs where a slim patch of smooth skin peeked out from the silk robe. Jimmy coughed and presented Ellen the newspaper.

"The daily paper as requested."

Ellen accepted it and strolled over to her nightstand to retrieve her purse for a tip. Jimmy allowed himself the luxury of inhaling her perfumed scent while his eyes bathed in her voluptuous curves. She extracted a dollar bill and turned back toward him.

Jimmy straightened up, eyes forward in anticipation of the tip.

"Thank you Miss Ellen. This is much appreciated."

"Nonsense, Jimmy. You go out of your way to bring me the paper." She noticed he was lingering. "Anything else I can do for you?"

Jimmy clutched his hat and turned his head both ways to make sure no one else was around. "You might want to look at the cover. I can't read but I think you might find it interesting."

Ellen unfolded the tabloid and feasted her eyes on a most unappealing photo of herself. The headline read: Naïve youth funds Nazi gathering

The photo had been taken when she first appeared and had been caught off-guard by the camera flashes. It was also blurry and unflattering.

She hurled the paper across the room.

"Those rats!"

The daily rag was operated by a corporation of tight fisted conservatives, many of whom opposed America's entry into the summer games, fearful that they would lose Jewish sponsorship.

"Something wrong Miss Ellen?" Jimmy inquired, fearful that he might be involved in trouble.

She shook her head. "Nothing to trouble you Jimmy. I'm sure you've encountered your share of racists in this country. Someone out there doesn't want these athletes to compete in the Olympics and they're slandering my good intentions for their cause."

He nodded, pretending he understood. "So sorry, I know you are a champion for everyone Miss Ellen. My pappy says it runs in your blood. Your late Daddy was made of the same mettle."

"Thanks, Jimmy."

She opened the door indicating that he should leave. She was about to close it on him when he whirled and addressed her again.

"I almost forgot Miss Ellen. You asked me to keep an eye out for your privacy. Some gentleman in the lobby been asking about you. Name is Evans, I think. Has one of those big old cameras slung around his neck."

Ellen smiled. "Okay, Jimmy. See you tomorrow."

When the porter had departed, Ellen swiftly retrieved the crumpled newspaper and glared at the small print under the photo.

Picture by James Evans.

"James Evans, huh?" she whispered. "Looking for a follow up shoot I bet!"

Never one to back down from a challenge, Ellen raced to the bureau and quickly picked out clothing for the day. Mister James Evans would face the fury of her wrath this morning!

Dolled up in a flashy canary yellow sundress, Ellen Patrick strolled purposely into the expanse of the Hotel Roosevelt lobby. Immediately, a fellow sprung from one of the chairs in the pompous waiting area.

"Miss Patrick, please a word with you?"

Ellen turned seductively and took in his appearance. He was a square jawed, clean cut man dressed in a worn and wrinkled suit. It didn't detract from his handsome features.

"Are you talking to me?"

The man caught his breath and removed his hat. His wavy black hair was clean but in need of a trim.

"I'm sorry to ambush you like this, but ..."

"Sorry?" Ellen interrupted, "Whatever for?" She didn't give him a chance to answer. "That's a fine camera you have there, must belong to a professional."

Evans rubbed at his nose. "Well, now that you mention it..."

She cut him off again. "Of course you couldn't be a professional."

"Why do you say that?" He inquired, struck with genuine confusion.

Ellen changed her breezy expression to a grimace.

"Because I've seen your shoddy work, Mister James Evans!"

The embarrassed photographer turned red. "Actually, that's why I'm here. I wanted to apologize for the photo they ran on the cover this morning."

"I'm listening."

Evans fondled his camera. "It was never my intention to humiliate you. I never would have turned in that shot if I was aware of it. Truth is I dropped the film off at the publisher late last night, and he selected that shot." He paused. "I am truly sorry."

"You were just trying to make a living."

His mood turned sour. "But not at your expense. I take pride in my work, Miss Patrick. I'm no dummy. The paper is controlled by vultures who answer to even bigger maggots. They deliberately are out to ruin your effort, and that ticks me off!"

Ellen calmed down; any need for a battle had left her mind the minute she had spotted this gent in his worn-out suit. He was another rube being played by money hoarders who shoveled rumors and innuendo to a public desperate and thirsty for any thing to distract them from a struggling economy.

It had got so bad that guards were actually stationed at California borders to prevent the influx of 'undesirables' all hoping to grab a piece of the American dream. Ellen found herself irate that hard working folks were being cheated out of their dough, swallowing whatever malarkey imaginative publishers fed them.

"I'm not mad at you Mister Evans."

She started to depart when he grabbed her arm. His touch was gentle, but she sensed a great strength within him.

"If it's all the same, it would sure make a guy feel better if I could make it up to you by buying you breakfast?"

Ellen smiled. She liked his boldness. Many men were intimidated by her wealth and social status, but James Evans likes to swing for the fence.

"I have a little time, Mister Evans before my first appointment. One of my favorite joints is on the way. "

He beamed and locked arms with her. "Lead the way Miss Patrick."

"Ellen."

"Beg your pardon?"

She swung around, locking her chocolate colored eyes on him. "If you're going to buy me a meal, you should at least address me by name."

He flashed a winning grin. "Consider it done, Ellen. I like to go by Jim. James is just for the photo credits."

"Jim, it is then."

She led him out of the glorious Roosevelt and out into the California sunshine, her mind distracted from the negative headlines.

Breakfast went off almost without a hitch. Ellen enjoyed a plate of ham and scrambled eggs, which helped combat some of the fatigue she was battling from too many champagne toasts. Jim Evans devoured a stack of buttermilk pancakes. The pair had chatted amiably during the meal, exchanging opinions regarding the upcoming games, and both fondly recalling the previous incantation.

Ellen found herself charmed by the brazen photographer. She even offered to let him shoot a calendar session she was doing for charity. The nosebleed crowd was appalled by Ellen's decision to pose in her bathing suit, but the buxom blonde was happy to do it as the proceeds would benefit the local YMCA.

When the waitress brought the bill, James Evan fished through his pockets, producing a handful of dimes. All newspaper folks carried handfuls of dimes. Ellen felt her heartbreak as he counted out change, coming up a few coins short.

"Let me get this." She whispered, not wanting to offend his honor.

James Evans grimaced. "No, I'm not hard-up or anything. I've got a voucher in for last night's work. Believe it or not, that rag pays well for a photo of someone as beautiful as you. That's why I was shocked when I saw that cover today."

Ellen ignored his banter and slipped the loose change from her purse onto the table when she thought he wasn't looking. Evans swallowed his pride and pretended not to notice. He sorted out the correct amount and left a healthy tip.

"Am I being too forward in asking you to dinner tonight?" He asked.

Ellen dabbed at her lips with a napkin.

"Not at all James, but I must take a rain check. The German entourage is in town for only a few days, and I promised to chaperone the good Doctor to a number of our city's finest venues."

James Evans sighed. "Lucky dog travels continents and ends up spending the night with you. I envy him."

Ellen tapped a finger on his nose, her ample bosom straining against her sundress as she reached across the table.

"Be patient, Jim Evans. I have a feeling you have nothing to be jealous of."

He was thrilled by her recognition. "Say I have an idea. You need to drum up press for your Olympic sponsorship. Why don't you retain my services tonight? You know, capture a night out on the town with America's beauty hosting those uppity krauts."

She laughed. "James Evans, you are persistent. Just one thing…"

"Anything for you darling… Name it."

Ellen reached into her purse and grabbed a pen and paper. She jotted down an address before sliding the sheet across the table.

"What's this?"

She eyed him up and down.

"That's the location of a well- known tailor. If you want to join us tonight, you'd better hurry over there today and pick-up a new suit."

Evans frowned. He was about to protest when Ellen raised a hand.

"Not charity. It will come out of your pay. Trust me, handsome, you'll be glad you did."

With that, Ellen Patrick planted a kiss on his lips and swiveled her marvelous hips from the stool, leaving James Evans to count his blessings.

Later that evening, James Evans banged on the door of Ellen's suite. He was attired in a splendid dark blue suit, tailored for his physique. The expensive duds made him feel better about himself. He ran a finger across his teeth, worried that he may have remnants of a hot dog he had swallowed on the way over. Past experiences had taught him Ellen's social circle didn't subscribe to the same daily diet as a newspaper photographer. James Evans idea of a perfect meal was dropping two dimes for a loaf of bread and a pound of hamburg.

"Miss Patrick, it's me, Jim." He announced.

Ellen opened the door. She was wearing a bathrobe.

Evans cleared his throat.

"Come on in, Jim. Fix yourself a drink while I get dressed."

Evans entered the suite and tossed his hat across the room. It landed on the desk with ease. He spotted the ice bucket and glasses and helped himself to a shot of scotch.

"Should I pour you one?"

Ellen shook her head. "No, I have a feeling these Germans will try to ply me with booze tonight. No need to give them a head start."

Jim Evan shrugged and tossed back his liquor.

"The suit looks great on you." Ellen called from the bedroom.

Evans helped himself to a refill and then answered, "Yes, and to think all these years I didn't think I could afford one of those fancy stores on the boulevard."

Ellen smiled. She neglected to tell him that she had phoned ahead and told her friend, Pierre the tailor, to minimize the charge and she'd cover the difference.

She disrobed and selected a long flowing white dress. She dressed swiftly, eager to rejoin the photographer's company. The final item of clothing was a pair of white high-heeled stilettos. Satisfied with her appearance, she emerged from the bedroom.

Evans took a gander at her plunging neckline and almost dropped his glass. He whistled a wolf call. "Va-va-voom!"

"Stop it!" Ellen kidded. "You're supposed to be working for me tonight." She glided over to him and fixed his tie. He could feel her hot breath. It drove him wild. "Speaking of which, did you forget something?"

Evans looked at her queerly. His face flushed and his hands dropped to his fly. Much to his relief, he had not left it open. Confused, he shrugged.

"Beats me," and then he squinted his eyes in agony, "my camera!"

Ellen squeezed his nose. "What type of lensman are you? Forgetting your tools?"

Sheepishly, he grabbed his hat.

"I left it my car. I'll run down and be back in a jiffy."

"Ok." Ellen responded. She watched him exit the room, amused at his embarrassment. She strolled over to the desk and retrieved her purse. She emptied the contents on the smooth surface. It contained the usual feminine accoutrements- lipstick, make-up, safety pins, etc. A she also carried a shiny new lighter, a 'zippo' they had called it, a gift from one of the nightclub owners.

At the bottom of her purse, lay the interesting articles, a black domino mask, a .22 automatic and a stack of business cards. These items belonged to her other persona, the crime fighting heroine better known as The Domino Lady.

It was a beautiful spring evening in sunny California, and Ellen had left the door of her terrace balcony open. Her keen ears detected a commotion going on down below. The Roosevelt was known for being very discreet, and many a street urchin was handled roughly by the overzealous doormen. Her intuition told her this was anything but an ordinary street scuffle.

Ellen allowed her eyes to drift over the scene taking place on the sidewalk below. Her excellent vision immediately spotted the German entourage in the midst of the argument. She could see Doctor Franz Hinnenburg in the melee. He towered over the other combatants.

At the bottom of her purse, lay the interesting articles...

She could also see the bright flash cubes popping off all around them. "Jim!"

Quickly donning her mask, Ellen slipped her gun into her garters and bolted out of the room. She opted for the stairs knowing she could outpace the elevator without becoming winded. At the bottom of the stairs, she slammed into the emergency exit door and rushed toward the battle.

The Domino Lady plunged into combat immediately.

The Germans were being attacked by a quartet of black masked men, armed with wooden baseball bats. Only Franz Hinnenburg seemed to fare well against his attackers. The gigantic man slammed one of his opponents to the pavement. The man grunted, dazed but not seriously hurt.

Out of the corner of her eye, Domino Lady glimpsed James Evans snapping photos of the battle royal. His back was turned to one of the masked men who was about to put him in a choke hold when Domino Lady sprang into action. She drove a spiked heel deep into the man's spine, causing him to scream in agony. He tried to circle and get a grip on her, but she eluded his grasp and finished him off with an elbow to his neck. He would not be waking soon.

Sensing a new obstacle to their attack, two of the other combatants rushed toward Domino Lady. She simply somersaulted over them, and before they knew it she was behind them. Two quick judo chops put those villains out of commission.

Domino Lady turned to help Franz Hinnenburg with the last of the attackers, but the masked man had sensed that the tide of the battle had turned against his favor. He withdrew a revolver and aimed it at the doctor. Domino Lady was too far away to intervene.

"Doctor!" she yelled helplessly.

In the instant before the gunman fired, James Evans had thrown himself in front of the German. The bullet intended for Franz Hinnenburg slammed into James Evans' body, lifting him off the ground. The photographer's eyes locked with Domino Lady's and she could have sworn he mouthed the word "sorry" before he crumbled in a heap to the sidewalk.

The emotionless gunman reacted instinctively, shoving Franz Hinnenburg into the back of an idling car. Domino Lady was about to resume her attack, when she heard James Evans moaning.

"Help me!" The bleeding photographer pleaded.

Domino Lady watched helplessly as the getaway car peeled away from the curb in a cloud of smoke and burnt rubber.

She rushed over to the wounded photographer. There was a pool of blood floating around him. His eyes were closed, and his breathing was labored, but he still lived.

"Someone call an ambulance!" Domino Lady barked into the throng of onlookers that had developed. She cradled James Evans' head in her lap, oblivious to the large blood stains he left on her dress.

"Don't you give up on me Jim Evans!"

The photographer opened his eyes. Groggy, he drank in Domino Lady's appearance. A wide grin formed on his face.

"An angel! If I knew they looked like you …"

He didn't finish his thought, darkness overtaking him.

Domino Lady didn't stick around for the police. Vigilantes were frowned upon in the city by the men in blue, many of whom were under mob control. With a heavy heart, Domino Lady watched from the shadows as the medical attendants roared away from the scene in their ambulance, siren blaring.

She returned to the comfort of her hotel room to compose a plan of action.

Tears welled in her eyes as she removed the blood stained dress.

"Poor Jim!"

Despite having just met him, she felt a strong intensity toward the go-getter. Ellen had always topped the society pages' list of most desirable women and she lacked no quantity of would be suitors, ranging from politicians, to athletes, and even mobsters had sought her attention, but Ellen had never been smitten like she was with James Evans. There was just something so down-to-earth about him that reminded her of her late father.

"Why me?" She asked herself.

A strong resolve settled over her, much like it had in the aftermath of her father's murder. Ellen didn't believe in pity or sorrow. She believed in action. That was how the Domino Lady had emerged. She knew her father wouldn't approve of her sitting around, pining at her loss. He had raised her to be brave and combat adversity.

She'd get through this, and so would James Evans. Right now, she was powerless to help him. Only the surgeons could mend his wounds. Ellen had other priorities right now. A German diplomat was missing and she had to find him before an international crisis erupted.

One of the benefits of being in the social spotlight, a person was able to establish valuable contacts in the outside world. Ellen Patrick had obtained such a tool in the form of Detective William O'Leary, a rugged Irish dick that she had more than a casual acquaintance with. As she dialed his number, she wished the circumstances were better.

It took the station a few moments to transfer her call, but she recognized her friend's thick brough as he bellowed a greeting into the receiver.

'Ellen, lassie, now is not a good time. I'm up to me ears in caseloads, and the chief just dumped a shooting down at the Roosevelt on me."

She cleared her throat.

"Believe it or not that's where I'm calling you from. I saw the whole thing from my balcony window."

The burly Irishman grabbed for his paper and pen.

'You don't say? Then you must know that sultry siren, the Domino Lady, was spotted at the scene. Seems she shows up wherever trouble is lately."

"Was she now? " Ellen asked innocently. She suspected detective O'Leary might be implying something with his tone.

"It be true. That she-devil must have first-hand knowledge of crimes to be so quick at the scene."

Ellen snapped, "Or maybe she's just good at what she does?"

"Don't' make a fuss, darling. I admit what she does crosses the boundaries of justice, but someone had to make a stand against the scumbags that infiltrated this once proud city. Not since your late departed daddy has someone stuck up for the little people like she has. Want to know a secret?"

"What's that?" Ellen asked breathlessly.

"The uniforms might be jealous of her nabbing all their collars for them, but deep down they appreciate her getting the dirty jobs done. Imagine, a woman, a beautiful one at that, taking on mobsters. Saint's alive!"

Ellen changed the subject.

"Can you tell me anything about the case?"

William O'Leary let of huge guffaw.

"Pretty, lady, you know I can't divulge police business!"

'Please, Billy, for me... for what we once were."

O'Leary was silent.

"Billy, you're not still angry with me?"

"Nah! Well maybe a little."

Ellen, or more correctly, Domino Lady had foiled a loan shark operation that O'Leary had spent two weeks undercover working on. The big man had not taken it well. His disappointment had lingered to the point where the couple broke it off.

"Billy?"

"You know I can't stay mad at you, sweet lady. We're holding three of those guys in lockup right now. I haven't had a chance to question them."

Ellen released her breath. She hadn't realized she was holding it.

"Any word on the German? I watched them hustle him into a getaway car."

"Nothing yet..."

There was a brief moment of silence and then a commotion in the squad room. Ellen could hear William O'Leary dumping articles from his desk as he bolted from his chair.

"What's happening?" She demanded.

She received no reply, just the jumbled sounds of confusion and yelling in the precinct. Ellen strained her ears to listen. Her keen mind tried to filter out the background noise and focus on the gruff voice of Detective O'Leary.

"All dead!" She heard the big man shout.

Voices filtered through her mind, but she heard one word standout.

Cyanide!

The masked men who had been involved in the shooting of James Evans and the abduction of Doctor Franz Hinnenburg were dead, suicide victims of cyanide poisoning.

Ellen slammed down the phone receiver, time to visit the hospital.

Ellen packed a small travel bag containing her Domino Lady gear and headed down to County General. Opened only a few years ago, the medical facility was quickly establishing a reputation as one of the best in the country. James Evans chances of survival had just increased.

She greeted a small throng of policemen and reporters outside the photographer's room. He had been settled into the intensive care unit, the doctors having done their best to patch him up. His fate stood in higher hands now.

One of the young medics recognized Ellen from one of her previous visits to the hospital. She frequently visited the children's unit, showering them with gifts and doing her part to ease their suffering. The young surgeon, David Carson, looked fragile.

Los Angles had become a breeding ground of corruption. The emergency wards were constantly filled with victims of underworld violence, not to mention the population inflicted with the diseases of poverty and malnutrition. He had been on watch when James Evans was brought in.

"He took a bullet to the upper chest, Miss Patrick. It barely missed his heart and lungs, but he has lost quite a bit of blood. The good news is he is young and strong. I'm giving him a fighting shot at pulling through."

Ellen was thankful for this news.

"Is he awake?"

The young doctor shook his head.

"The men in blue have been waiting for a statement, but he keeps drifting in and out. I can't let them keep grilling him."

Ellen pleaded, "Can I talk to him?"

"Probably not a good idea."

"Tears welled up in her eyes.

The young doctor folded. "If it was anyone else, but you... go ahead in. Five minutes, tops. Agreed?"

Ellen hugged him. "You're the best, doc."

She glided past the throng of officers and into the room. James Evans lay on his back, a bit pale and very still. Ellen felt a surge of anger flow through her.

Why? Why do we put up with this?

The recession had turned a once rebel country into a land of opportunists who preyed on hard working Americans like James Evans.

Only as the Domino Lady was Ellen able to confront these criminals and administer justice in a stern way.

Evans' nose twitched.

"I know that perfume." He whispered.

"Jim, I'm so sorry."

"For what?"

"For not saving you."

The words came out before she could choke them back. If she wasn't careful she'd giveaway the identity of the Domino Lady.

"Funny."

"What is?"

"I had a dream an angel saved me. It was you, all dressed in white, but you wore a weird mask."

Ellen interrupted him. "That's the meds talking. You work the beat, you must have heard about the Domino Lady?"

"That babe that goes around wiping out mobsters? Who hasn't?"

Inwardly, Ellen beamed. "She was your angel."

"You don't say?"

"Jim, they took Doctor Hinnenburg. Those masked men."

"Not good, the krauts will be furious."

"Do you remember anything that will help?"

He thought hard, "On the table."

"What?"

"My camera... Take it to the Daily. Ask for Donovan. You can trust him. He'll develop the role."

Ellen nodded. "Is there anything I can do for you?"

"A kiss would make it better."

She giggled. "I promise better than that when you drag yourself out of that bed." She kissed him on the forehead. "Promise me you'll do what the doctor says?"

"Scouts' honor."

"You were a boy scout?"

"Where do you think I learned how to focus a camera? Now go on and get that film to Donovan."

Ellen grabbed the camera off the table and headed to the elevator. It was late evening but newspapers didn't close shop. She had a feeling Donovan would still be on duty and she wanted the role of film developed, anything to take her mind off James Evans's condition.

The newsroom of the LA Daily was a bustle of activity, even at this late hour. Copy boys roamed the narrow spaces between desks filled with grizzled pencil pushers wearing fedoras and smoking cheap cigars. None of them missed a beat when Ellen Patrick wandered through on her way to the darkroom area.

She was greeted by an ogre-like stocky fellow who looked like he had torn all his hair out. His shiny bald head was offset by furry mutton chops running down the side of his face. He shook Ellen's hand vigorously.

"Miss Ellen Patrick, yesterday's cover girl!" He shouted above the newsroom turmoil.

"In the flesh."

Donovan puffed out his chest. He eyed Ellen up and down boldly. After what seemed like an eternity, he let out a thunderous howl.

"You were born for the camera!"

Frustrated, Ellen slammed Jim Evans' camera into the man's large belly. He pushed out an exaggerated breath.

"Guess, I deserved that. Jimmy didn't give me all the particulars, just that he had been winged by a stray bullet while snapping photos outside the Roosevelt."

"Winged?" Ellen snapped. "He was shot in the chest. I just left his bed at County General."

Donovan glared at his timepiece. "I know. Don't worry, he's a tough kid. I bet Jimmy will be out of that place in no time. Important thing is that you got this film here in time for tomorrow's early edition."

Ellen poked a finger at the big man. "I really don't care about your deadline. I want a copy of those photos as fast as you can!"

"Whoa! Easy young lady! It takes time."

Ellen forced herself to show restraint, fearful that the Domino Lady might be exposed. She had to maintain her image as a young socialite.

"Forgive my histrionics, Mr. Donovan. James is my employee now, and I feel terrible that this took place during his time with me. I know this shoot will earn him some extra dollars."

Relaxed, Donovan fondled the camera.

"Ironic, huh?"

"What is sir?"

He pointed at the camera. "That he was taking photos of the Germans."

Ellen frowned. "I don't follow."

"Jimmy and me, we make our living with cameras and Germany is the camera kingdom of the world. The most popular brands Leica and Contrax are German made in Stuttgart."

"Really?" her impatience was starting to wear thin.

"Oh yes," Donovan continued, "Want to know a secret? Even though they would deny it, Kodak was also founded by Germans."

Ellen couldn't take it anymore. "Fascinating, Mike, do you mind if I look around while you develop the photos?"

"Not at all, pretty lady, but stay away from the printing rollers. You will get so crushed you'll be turned into a human postage stamp!"

Ellen flashed her best effort at a smile and strolled off. It was getting late, and she sought out a cup of coffee. She was halfway to the break room when a copy boy came barreling down the path. His eyes betrayed his frantic efforts to get by her.

"Easy young man, where's the fire?"

The youth halted, drawing in deep breaths of air.

"Sorry, lady, I gotta get this to the chief immediately!"

"Must be important?"

The teen stopped, noticing her for the first time. His eyes traveled up and down the contours of her body and his knees started to tremble.

"Oh my gosh!" He stammered. "Ellen Patrick! It's a pleasure to meet me!" He slapped his forehead. "I mean you. To meet you."

Ellen pointed at his notes. "Headline stuff I bet?"

"For sure! Didn't you hear?" He didn't wait for an answer. "They found that German doctor. Hindenburg."

"You mean Hinnenburg?"

The youth nodded, "Right, like I said they found him, or what was left of him. Someone found his charred body down by the pier!"

Ellen felt sick. "Do they know who did it?"

"Nope, but the killers left a note."

'What did it say?"

The youth turned hesitantly. "You ain't gonna flap this all over town?" He whispered. "I would get canned, and my mom would toss me out."

Ellen placed a hand over her heart. "Our secret!"

The teen stretched his neck in every direction to make sure no one was listening.

"Only for you, Miss Patrick. "

She nodded in agreement. "Go ahead."

He cleared his throat. "It read, get out of our country!"

Ellen closed her eyes. This was a disaster. The international world would be in an upheaval. Franz Hinnenburg, respected scientist, and ambassador for the Olympic games murdered on United States soil. This would not sit well with the powerful men of Berlin.

Ellen phoned police headquarters. She was immediately patched through to William O'Leary. She could sense the urgency in his usually confident demeanor.

"You saved me the effort of sending out a search party." He confessed. "Washington is flying in some fancy pants boys to investigate this incident."

Ellen interrupted, "It's true, then?"

"Sadly, yes. A couple of derelicts came across the body a short time ago. The body was burned up but the killers were kind enough to leave his identification papers nearby. Money was still in the billfold."

"The foreign press will eat this up." Ellen mumbled, mostly for her own benefit.

O'Leary felt her pain. "Don't blame yourself, lassie. These German men knew what might happen when they entered our country. Times are tough, and the blather coming out of their traps about superiority, well that don't sit well with a bunch of hungry Americans."

"That's not an excuse for murder!" She sniped.

"I'll have to agree with you there. Thing is, the commissioner doesn't want any part of this."

Ellen was confused. "What do you mean?"

"The Germans are demanding I release the body to them right now. They are disgusted by our lack of authority and want to return to the homeland immediately."

"Billy, we can't let that happen! The foreign press will crucify our city. It could lead to America's expulsion from the games."

"Sister, it could lead to a hell of a lot more than that."

"Like what?"

"Those boys over there are just itching for a real brawl. This might be just the ticket to incite an uproar."

Ellen was shocked.

"Billy, are you suggesting this could put our countries at war?"

O'Leary didn't hesitate. "Now you follow me. That's why I need to solve this quickly. Show them that America doesn't show favoritism when it comes to justice."

"You need to stall them, Billy."

"I agree, but I don't know how long that can last. The fellows are trying to get a flight out of here as we speak, and the suits in Washington demand we turn the investigation over to them as soon as they arrive. Time is our enemy, Ellen."

"I'm waiting on some photos. Just keep the body away from everyone."

"How do I do that?"

"Procedure, Billy."

"I don't follow, girl."

Ellen gritted her teeth. "Follow procedure. Don't release that body until every last speck of paperwork is accounted for."

The burly Irishman bellowed. "I think I follow, lassie. We'll give them the runaround, but unless a miracle drops in our lap soon, we're gonna have egg on our face."

Ellen hung up with a sense of urgency. She rushed from the newsroom back to the paper's darkroom.

Ellen finally grabbed a coffee. It was weak and burnt, and it tasted delicious. She gulped a couple of mouthfuls before tossing the remainder. Mike Donovan was still processing the role of film. She wasn't sure it would be helpful. The masked men who had committed suicide still hadn't been identified. She was grasping at straws.

"Hey, Miss Patrick!"

It was the copy boy from earlier.

Ellen smiled. "Must have been exciting delivering that big headline to the chief?"

The boy shrugged. "You would think?"

"What happened?" she asked curiously.

"Big Moe, that's the chief, Moe Bernstein. He ain't a fan of the krauts. He said it was a back page story at best."

Ellen was confused. "Why would he say that?"

A deep voice from the doorway answered her.

"Why don't you ask him yourself?"

In the shadow of the doorway stood a gruff man of about sixty with a crisp white shirt and suspenders. Ellen recognized him from some previous social event. He was Moe Bernstein, editor in chief of the Daily.

"Mister Bernstein, I'm Ellen…"

He cut her short. "I know who you are Miss Patrick. I do read my paper. I apologize for that photograph."

"It didn't bother me as much as the caption."

Moe Bernstein shooed the copy boy away and sat down next to Ellen. She could smell a faint body odor masked with cologne.

"I respected your father."

Ellen raised an eyebrow. "But not the child?"

"Miss Patrick, that young boy that left here? I was his age once. I hustled

"Why don't you ask him yourself?"

up and down these hallways, breaking my tail, until one day I hit the corner office and settled in."

"I'm aware of your success story." Ellen conceded. "That's why I find your bias so disturbing."

Bernstein's face turned red. "These men are frauds! They say they come here to promote goodwill. They only promote themselves. "

"The Olympics transcend politics, sir. Doctor Hinnenburg, he…"

The editor sprung from his chair.

"Doctor? Butcher, more likely. I will not make him a martyr! "

Ellen stood toe to toe. "He was murdered!"

"Good!" Bernstein shouted. "Serves him right. All his talk of Aryan supermen and inferior races. Whoever did this, I salute them!"

Ellen was at a loss for words.

"Murder is never acceptable."

Bernstein grabbed both her hands. "Dear child, listen to yourself! You father was a noble man of values struck down long before his time. Don't deny you haven't imagined horrible fates for his killers?"

She lowered her eyes. Ellen Patrick had only imagined such acts, but the Domino Lady had struck down many foes in her quest for justice.

"You are young, Miss Patrick. Turn your energy to other endeavors. Forget these silly games. Let these men leave our land in fear. They will not find America easy prey."

Bernstein departed abruptly. Ellen found herself questioning if the editor knew who may have orchestrated the murder. Her thoughts were interrupted by the return of Mike Donovan. He carried a large envelope containing the developed film. She thanked him and headed back to her hotel room.

Ellen Patrick studied the photographs from the comfort of her hotel's bath tub. The steaming water soothed her nerves as she sorted through the stack Mike Donovan had developed. Much to her relief, the Domino Lady did not appear in any of the shots.

James Evans had snapped off a dozen photos of the brawl, unfortunately most of them blurry or out of focus. The few decent shots revealed no new information. The getaway car had evaded James Evans notice.

"Probably stolen anyway." She mused.

There was nothing particularly glaring about the four masked attackers. They wore standard ski masks that could have been purchased at any local Army surplus store. There were no markings or adornments that tied them to any cause.

She flipped through the stack again, concentrating on the intended target, Franz Hinnenburg. The tall German looked stoic in the shots, seemingly unfazed by the attack. Ellen recalled him hurling one of the masked men to the sidewalk. He had done it effortlessly for a man so intent on proclaiming himself physically handicapped from a war injury. Still, he was so broad shouldered and masculine, she hadn't questioned his heroics at all. She just got a bad vibe about it.

"Why the fisticuffs? They had guns." She puzzled.

Four armed men should have been a deterrent for resistance, yet Doctor Hinnenburg had fought them off with ease. It reminded her of a staged production, only James Evans had been the wildcard. The photographer had interrupted a rehearsed scene.

The in-room phone rang, startling her.

Ellen raced across the room, soap and water dripping from her naked body.

William O'Leary's voice echoed through the handset.

"The feds are here, Ellen. I was able to shake them off for now, but a few calls to my commish and I'll have to hand over Hinnenburg's remains. They want to avoid a scene with Berlin so they're going to hand the body over to the krauts and escort them directly to the airport."

"Where is the body now?"

"Still at the morgue. The medical examiner hasn't touched it. He don't want no part of this circus!"

Ellen detected the urgency in her friend's voice.

"Hang in there Billy! I'm going to contact a friend and see if she can help."

O'Leary grinned. "Ye wouldn't be referring to a certain spotlight grabbing vigilante we both know? Officially, the LAPD must caution against individuals who take the law into their own hands, but off the record, that heavenly avenger may be this country's only hope!"

"Just keep stalling! The Domino Lady is on her way!"

Ellen slammed down the receiver and toweled herself dry. Domino Lady's bloody dress still hung draped over the chair, but fortunately she had packed another. She dressed as quickly as possible, donning the familiar costume. She always felt empowered wearing it. The silk fabric and shiny nylons oozed femininity, while the black domino mask suggested mystery and intrigue. Her long golden locks hinted at the power of a lioness.

She allowed herself the extra minute to apply lipstick, a liberty that raised her level of confidence.

Admiring herself in the mirror, she whispered, "Ready or not…"

Ellen had phoned down to the lobby. The crusty concierge who answered was shocked when she had requested to speak with Jimmy, the porter. The racist old man's mind boggled with impure suggestions, but he was a cautious businessman. He politely asked Ellen to remain on the line while he tracked the boy down.

A moment later, the dark skinned youth picked up the receiver.

"Hollywood Roosevelt, this is Jimmy." He uttered in his most professional voice.

"Jimmy, it's Ellen Patrick."

The youth relaxed. He knew Ellen would cause him no harm.

"Yes, Miss? May I bring you a paper or a cocktail perhaps?"

Ellen cut him off. "Listen carefully, Jimmy. I need a favor, a big one."

Jimmy spied the concierge glaring at him. The man was out of earshot, but Jimmy turned his back cautiously.

"Anything for you, ma'am."

His sincerity was evident. Ellen knew the boy didn't have a bad bone in his body.

"Jimmy, I have a friend who needs a car immediately. Nothing fancy, nothing that will be missed. I will take full responsibility for any damages that may occur."

The boy was confused.

"Why don't I bring you yours?"

"This is a private matter, Jimmy. No one can know about it. Can you get me a car in the next five minutes?"

The youth flashed a wide smile.

"I'll have it on the west corner in two minutes."

"Thanks, Jimmy. You're the best."

The boy panicked. "Miss Ellen, how will I know your friend?"

"Trust me Jimmy. You will recognize her!"

Jimmy the Porter had secured a vehicle with haste. He carefully selected a non-descript car belonging to the frisky daughter of a local entrepreneur who spent many an evening shacked up with her married boyfriend. The young woman would not report the car missing if she happened to venture out for a break from her steamy romance.

Domino Lady emerged from the dark shadows as Jimmy pulled up. It was past midnight and foot traffic was scarce. The few stragglers out for a walk didn't notice her, but the star struck youth most certainly did.

"Mama save me!" he whispered before whistling.

Domino Lady didn't speak. She simply extended her hand, wiggling the fingers.

Jimmy acknowledged by exiting the vehicle. His eyes stared unblinking.

"Miss Ellen didn't say it would be you!"

Domino Lady glided effortlessly behind the wheel, she rolled down the window before shifting into drive. She blew Jimmy a kiss and waved before peeling away from the sidewalk on her way to the morgue.

Jimmy watched until the car was out of view. He didn't realize his teeth were chattering. He had removed his uniform cap and had been gripping it so tight his fingers went numb.

"Wow!" He muttered, before turning back in the direction of the Roosevelt. "Yes, sir, the Lord was on his A-game the day he created her. Amen!"

Puffing out his chest, he entered the lobby, tipped his hat at the concierge, ignored the returning death gaze, and resumed his position in the lobby, a permanent smile affixed on his face.

Domino Lady tore through the downtown streets of Los Angeles, relying on her uncanny reflexes to guide her around the hazardous obstacles. Jimmy had procured a decent vehicle, the body was nothing special, but the tires were new, and Domino Lady tested them to the limit. Landmarks and tourist sights zoomed past her window. Within minutes, she was pulling up to the parking lot of the county morgue.

Domino Lady slammed on the brakes.

A black hearse was idling in front of the entrance, its back doors open. Domino Lady recognized some of the men mulling around. They were part of Hinnenburg's traveling entourage. They stood somber, playing the role of grieving friends.

Domino Lady also took note of a dark sedan parked next to it. Two dark suited men stood at attention, their backs to the hearse. Both wore scowls and matching close cropped hair.

"G-men!" She acknowledged.

Domino Lady calculated her chances of roaring into action and decided it would be wise to hold back. The federal escorts were too attentive and currently held the upper-hand. Besides, they were agents of the United States, men just doing their job. She wished to avoid gunplay with them.

Turning off the car's headlights, Domino Lady watched as the Germans emerged from the building with a body bag, undoubtedly the remains of Franz Hinnenburg. There would be no autopsy or documentation needed for them to depart the country. The feds would probably declare diplomatic immunity or some such red tape to bypass customary procedure. In fact, a plane was most likely on the tarmac already.

The Germans secured the hearse and entered it. The feds followed suit in the sedan. The two vehicles revved up and departed the morgue parking lot.

Domino Lady ducked down, her pale skin and silky white dress were not ideal for stealth missions. She counted slowly to five and pulled out after the two cars. She didn't bother turning on her headlights.

She wasn't surprised that the feds had declined a police escort. The men in blue would have insisted on sirens, and that would have drawn attention. The last thing the big wigs in Washington wanted was more press and photographers, which L.A. had no shortage of.

The two vehicles proceeded westbound in the direction of the airport.

Domino Lady followed, determination etched on her beautiful face. Call it instinct, feminine intuition, or just a plain old hunch, but Domino Lady sensed something wasn't right about this caper. If she was wrong, it would be more than just egg on her face, but she felt the risks outweighed the consequences of giving the Nazi party more ammunition in their war of propaganda.

It wasn't difficult giving chase without headlights. Los Angeles was lit up. Despite the nation's poverty and slow recovery from recession, the west coast had emerged more lucrative than before. The bright lights and luster of Hollywood worked in two different ways. Some saw the emerging movie business as a healthy distraction from the hunger and suffering the populace struggled through, while other more cynical parties felt the opulence and wealth was nothing more than a slap in the face to the common man.

Ellen Patrick was an optimist. That was why she supported the Olympic movement. The previous games had served as a triumphant symbol of American ingenuity while helping ease a burdened nation. The distraction, however small, had instilled a sense of pride and hope unseen for years. Ellen truly believed, win or lose, a strong American presence in Berlin would serve as a boost for the stagnant economy, but more importantly serve as a springboard for hope and inspiration.

With this in mind, she gripped the steering wheel tighter. The roads were uncongested and the airport would soon be in sight. Domino Lady needed to act now.

Domino Lady slammed her foot to the pedal. The hearse was too far out in front to try and cut it off, but the federal agents' sedan lulled peacefully in front of her. As she inched closer, an idea sprung to mind. She calculated her timing, knowing that any mishap could lead to fatalities.

As she pulled within inches of the moving vehicle, Domino Lady flipped on her headlights, blinding the driver. She then sped up alongside the dark sedan and with a quick flick of her wrist slammed the edge of her vehicle into the rear tire of the agents' car. Immediately, the driver spun in circles, as he tried to prevent fish-tailing the Sedan. Unfortunately, his reflexes caused him to slam on the brakes.

That action proved to be disastrous. The agents' vehicle spun in circles before gravity took over and the car began to roll. Domino Lady watched as the sedan skidded over a curb and wrecked against a brick wall. She gulped with anxiety, holding her breath until she saw both men emerge unscathed.

With that business taken care of, Domino Lady focused her attention on the hearse. Much to her surprise, the Germans were unaware of what had just happened. Assuming the federal agents had been in a fender bender, the German driver slowed down. This gave Domino Lady time to plan a form of action.

Domino Lady unholstered her .22 automatic, and leaning out the window of her moving vehicle was able to rip a shot off at the tires on the hearse. Her aim was perfect, and the rubber exploded on impact. Fortunately, the car had been drifting slowly so no one was injured.

Domino Lady slammed on her brakes and ran up to the hearse. She rapped with the butt of her automatic on the window. An ashen faced German rolled it down. His manner was robotic. He was in shock.

"Turn that engine off now!" Domino Lady ordered.

She didn't have to ask twice. The man's companion sat quietly, cringing at Domino Lady's voice. Truth was he was terrified of the vision in white who had the barrel of a gun pointed in his direction.

"Don't hurt us lady!" The thug pleaded.

Domino Lady reached in and grabbed the car keys from the ignition. She reared back and hurled them across the street. She then grabbed the collar of the driver and yanked him from the seat. He didn't resist.

"Here is how this is going to play out." She commanded. "You two are going to load that body bag into my car right now. I don't want to hear any complaints!"

Neither man responded verbally. They moved like jack rabbits to vacate the vehicle. Domino Lady watched with satisfaction as they unloaded the good doctor's remains from the hearse. Everything was going according to plan until she felt a hot buzz skip by her shoulder.

"Bullets!" She moaned.

From down the street, the federal agents had regained their composure and were headed toward the hearse, guns blazing. Domino Lady somersaulted over the opened car door for protection. A spectacular trick in high heels. Her movement had saved her life as hot lead ripped into the vehicle's frame.

"Stop in the name of the law!" One of the agents ordered.

Domino Lady motioned for the two Germans to get on the ground. No need to involve bystanders in a gunfight if one was to take place. Every fiber of her being wanted to retaliate against these armed foes, but her judgment prevailed.

She would not fire upon American agents. It was against her code of ethics. The gig was up. The Domino Lady would have to surrender!

A million thoughts raced through Domino Lady's head as the two agents scampered closer. What would people think? Ellen Patrick, darling of society, exposed as the notorious vigilante, the Domino Lady. Her reputation would be ruined, but more importantly her crusade for justice would come to a halt. She gritted her teeth, stopping herself from raising her weapon.

"Put that gun down right now! We know you're the Domino Lady. We will shoot to kill!"

Domino Lady cautiously lowered her gun to the ground. The men rumbled even closer. In another minute it would be over.

Suddenly a police cruiser roared upon the scene, traveling way too fast under the circumstances. The driver appeared to be steering out of control as he headed straight in the direction of the two federal agents, hand rapping on the horn frantically for them to move out of his way.

The two men instinctively stumbled for the sidewalk, unaware that the driver had intentionally planned to block off their access to the Domino Lady.

Unknown to them, the car was driven by Detective William O'Leary. The big Irish dick drove around the hearse and rolled down his window so Ellen could make out his features.

"O'Leary?" Domino Lady muttered with astonishment.

"Wipe off that crazy look sweetheart. You only got seconds to load that body into your vehicle and scram. "

Domino Lady was nervous. "Your career?"

The Irishman waved a hand. "Don't argue, I'll tell them a stray bullet sent me careening out of control. Just get jumping, sister!"

Domino Lady didn't hesitate. Mustering all her strength, she lifted the body bag herself into the rear door of her car. She slammed the door with gusto and waved a kiss at O'Leary.

"I owe you Detective."

"Call me Billy, doll. And this is a favor for some other blonde I know. Now scram!"

Domino Lady took one last look at the puzzled federal agents before slamming the gear shift into drive and peeling away from the scene. She was wanted now, and the streets would be crawling in search of the Domino Lady, but she had a plan.

She was going to gamble her entire load on a hunch. Leaving a cloud of smoke from the burning tire rubber, Domino Lady roared off in the direction of County General. In that beacon of hope lay her last chance to salvage the situation.

Doctor David Carson couldn't believe his eyes. He had just ended a sixteen hour day by successfully performing surgery on a young boy who had been struck by an ice cream truck earlier in the day. The boy's family had worried that the hospital would deny them care based on their meager income, but David Carson had rushed the boy from the emergency center into his operating room before the ink was dry on the admission papers.

The young surgeon treated all life with the same amount of respect and dignity, regardless of politics. That was why he stood transfixed at the lady in white who had summoned him to the parking garage. She looked tired and worn, but her beauty was undeniable.

"Do you know who I am?" Domino Lady asked.

"Yes," Carson responded, "News travels fast in a hospital. It seems you roughed up some federal agents and stole a corpse."

Domino Lady nodded. "Correct on both accounts. Listen Carson, I have it on good faith from a friend that you can be trusted?"

Carson smiled. "A certain blonde who bears a striking resemblance to you, perhaps?"

Domino Lady's pale skin flushed a deep hue of red.

"Yes, Ellen Patrick mentioned you. She said you saved the life of James Evans, the photographer."

Carson nodded. "I did. He peered into the backseat of the vehicle. "Appears I'm too late to save this one though."

"Yes, but you can help me save thousands more."

The doctor stared at the huge brown eyes peering out from the slits in her domino mask.

"Why would I help a fugitive?"

"Because you're a patriot and more importantly, you are a good man." Ellen stated. "This is the body purported to be Doctor Franz Hinnenburg."

"I am aware of that name. He was to appear at a charity function Miss Patrick threw tonight. I was invited but chose to save lives instead."

"I'm sure she values your contributions to society more than a financial donation."

Carson raised an eyebrow. "How would you know what she values?"

Domino Lady ignored his suggestive banter and cut to the chase.

"There are many people who want to sabotage the Olympic Games, both here and abroad. Some people are doing it for personal reasons such as our Jewish editor Moe Bernstein. I believe deep down, he may be right about the German intentions, but I don't think our citizens would stoop to killing an ambassador of the games."

"What do you think is going on?" asked Carson.

Domino Lady took a deep breath before responding. "I think this has been an elaborately planned hoax. I don't believe that Franz Hinnenburg can be found in that body bag. I suspect someone staged his kidnapping and murder."

"But why?"

"Political reasons. It would further the propaganda movement that Berlin seeks to branch out in their conquest of foreign lands. Imagine it, the Olympic ambassador slaughtered by jealous Americans only weeks before the games. This will cause unheralded outrage. The citizens of Germany will unite behind any cause for revenge."

Carson looked horrorfied.

"That's a bold assertion. Can you prove it?"

Domino Lady smiled. She tapped a slender finger against his hospital shirt.

"No, but you can."

Doctor David Carson shook his head in disbelief.

"Wait, you want me to do what?"

Domino Lady repeated her request.

"I want you to x-ray this corpse."

The young surgeon shook his head again, even harder.

"Why would I do that? This person is dead!"

The pair had removed the charred body from the black bag and placed it on a portable stretcher that Carson had wheeled down from the supply closet. They had draped the body with a bed sheet and Domino Lady had come up with the idea of adding a toe tag for authenticity. Carson had gone along with the ruse so far, but this request halted him in his tracks.

"Listen, Domino Lady, I don't care if you're a friend of Ellen Patrick or the mayor himself. What you're asking me to do is unethical."

Domino Lady remained calm. She explained her theory again.

"I don't believe this man is Doctor Hinnenburg. Sure, the height and weight are similar, but I have a feeling someone is trying to pull a fast one."

Carson peeked under the sheet.

"It will be near impossible to identify him. He's a foreigner. I'm sure dental records will be impossible to come by. Other than that, just look at him. The poor soul has been barbequed!"

Domino Lady snapped back the sheet, mostly to show him she meant business, but also to let the young man know she wasn't afraid.

"Doctor Hinnenburg was an athlete before entering the medical profession. A freak accident happened to him during his military service."

"Go on…" prompted the young doctor.

Domino Lady continued, "He shattered an ankle. Wouldn't that show up in his x-rays?"

Carson considered. "It may have healed nicely, but those type of injuries always leave remnants of bone damage. You just may have something!"

"Then you'll help me?"

The doctor laughed.

"I don't know if anyone can help you. Seriously, a mask and that flimsy dress? You call that a costume?"

Domino Lady remained silent.

Carson saw that she wasn't going to comment.

"I'm going to need time. My shift is over, and it will be highly unusual for me to go into the x-ray unit. Besides, the Domino Lady is a wanted criminal. Maybe it would be better if someone else showed up to help?"

Domino Lady smiled. "You refer to Ellen Patrick."

"Bingo. Meet me on the fifth floor. I'll get you your results."

Domino Lady threw herself at him impulsively, her soft lips brushing against the stubble on his cheeks. She whispered a thank you into his ear before vanishing from his sight.

Carson rolled his weary eyes and rolled up his sleeve. His sixteen hour shift had just been extended.

The Domino Lady transformed into Ellen Patrick effortlessly. The mask, automatic and garters had been shoved into a side pouch. She tied her hair up into a bun, and headed toward the hospital lobby. As she had anticipated, the place was a commotion.

The usual throng of injured folks mingled with press and uniformed officers. Ellen spotted the familiar face of William O'Leary in the thick of it. His jowls were flapping as he waved his hands re-enacting what must have been his interpretation of the incident with the feds. He was yakking at a group of suits who appeared angry with his explanation.

"Just cause you folks have jurisdiction don't mean you can come into this city and turn it upside down!" He bellowed.

The suits remained calm, snapping off questions rapidly at the big Irish

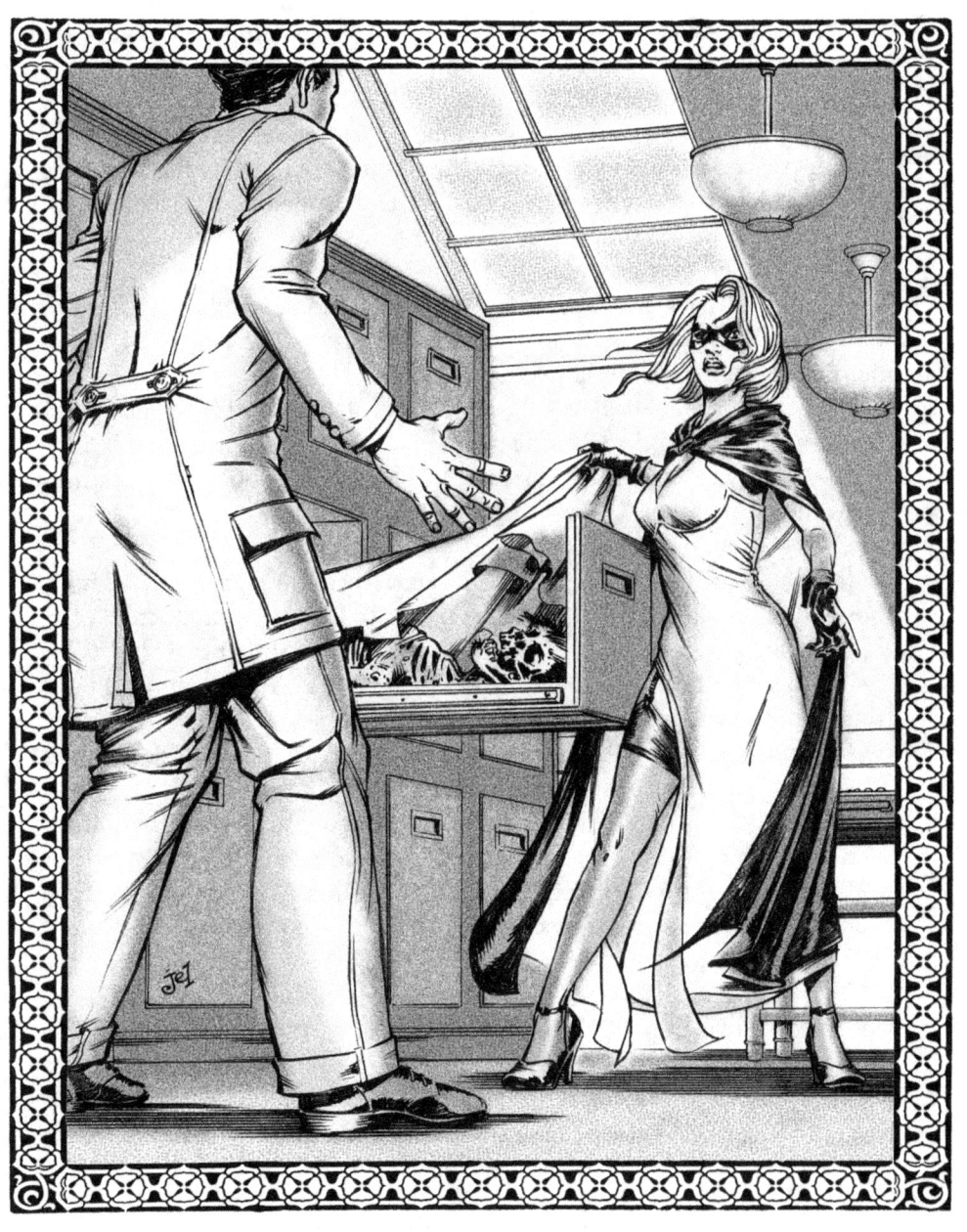

"He shattered an ankle. Wouldn't that show up in his x-rays?"

man. The angry dick answered each question as truthfully as possible. He knew his commissioner would punish him for the events that took place earlier, O'Leary didn't care. He suspected the commissioner was on the underworld's payroll, and because of that he had no respect for the man.

"The guy you should be grilling is Moe Bernstein down at the Daily. He hates these krauts more than any of us. If there's someone with a bloodlust out there, he'd be your man."

Ellen strolled over confidently.

"Good evening Detective." She smiled and shook hands with each of the agents. "Gentlemen, I'm Ellen Patrick. I was the late Doctor's host for his visit. It's terrible what happened to him."

One of the agents took a long look at her. His face didn't register recognition. He flipped through the pages of a notebook he was writing in.

"Don't stray too far, Miss Patrick. We need to ask you some questions about the kidnapping."

Ellen feigned fright.

"It terrifies me to recall such hideous acts. My photographer was shot by those hoodlums. I imagine they were trying to rob the good doctor."

The agent gave her a look of disinterest. He didn't bother to let her know the billfold had been found with the money intact. The agents had been trained not to let loose lips speak.

"I promise you we will sort this out, Miss Patrick. I must ask that you stay out of our proceedings until summoned. Is that clear?"

Ellen shook his hand. She made sure to hold on to it longer than necessary. She wanted to give the illusion of being star struck.

"Imagine being in the company of federal agents. My daddy would have been pleased. I'm sure you men will wrap this up in no time."

"Good night, Miss Patrick."

The agent turned his back to her, letting her know his time was too valuable to dawdle on a rich clueless child.

Pleased with herself, Ellen locked an arm around William O'Leary and dragged him to the elevator. The feds noticed but made no effort to stop the pair. Ellen wisely pressed the button for the sixth floor and waited for the doors to close.

Woosh!

As soon as the elevator began to lift, William O'Leary hugged her.

"Thanks kiddo. Those smug bums were really getting up my gander. They think they're so much better than we locals with their fancy college diplomas and expensive guns. I bet I could crack open all their heads faster than I crunch a walnut!"

Ellen laughed.

"Ignore those guys. The Domino Lady told me to inform you that she thanks you for aiding her escape."

"Don't have the slightest clue what you're talking about lassie. I was trying to be a municipal asset when I lost control of my vehicle during a pursuit of that voluptuous felon. Appears, she also outsmarted the feds. Tis a shame."

Ellen hugged him again.

"Billy, she was here. She dropped off the body with Dr. David Carson. He can be trusted."

O'Leary sighed. "Does it matter? What good is a doctor to a dead man, I ask?"

"If my hunch is right, Hinnenburg isn't dead"

"Don't be daft woman! I seen his burned up body myself. That man took his last breath some time ago,"

Ellen shook her head. "Not if that isn't him. I think the corpse is a plant. I'm not sure what their game is, but I think the Germans staged this entire episode."

O'Leary raised an eyebrow in disbelief.

"Then that would mean some other poor chap is in that body bag. Either way we have a murder on our hands!"

"The Domino Lady hopes to solve this caper tonight."

O'Leary nodded his agreement. It would thrill him to no end to stump the feds and as a bonus thwart a German escalation of war threat. The big Irishman knew only one woman was up to the task.

"What are we waiting for my lady? Lead on!"

Doctor Carson held the x-ray negative up to the light. Ellen Patrick and William O'Leary stared at it doubtfully. They exchanged quizzical looks with each other.

"Well, doc? What do you think?" Begged O'Leary.

Carson turned to Ellen with a smile on his lips.

"Your friend was correct. This isn't Franz Hinnenburg. This person has never broken an ankle."

Ellen hugged the doctor. She caught O'Leary sneering in the background. The big dick was jealous. She turned and hugged him also.

"Let me fetch the feds. I want to rub dirt in their face." O'Leary barked.

Ellen stifled him. "Hold your horses, Detective. This raises many new issues. "

The burly Irishman stopped dead in his tracks.

"A true killjoy you are!"

Ellen ignored him. She was back in Domino Lady mode.

"Why such an elaborate production? We already concluded the propaganda angle. So ask yourself this question, if this corpse isn't Franz Hinnenburg, why were the Germans in such a hurry to get it back to Germany?"

O'Leary formed a blank look. It was the young Doctor who answered.

"We were looking for signs of an old injury. Maybe we should have been looking for something else?"

Ellen grinned. O'Leary still expressed confusion.

"Someone fill me on what you two are cooking up! This whole shebang has left me with a headache."

Carson rolled up his sleeves again.

"I'll need you to exit the room." He ordered.

O'Leary was flabbergasted. "For heaven's sake why man?"

Ellen answered before the doctor could.

"So he can x-ray the rest of the body, Billy!"

Carson's suspicions proved fruitful. Inside the charred remains of the anonymous corpse lay several canisters of micro fiche. O'Leary ventured a guess immediately.

"Hidden documents. Probably blueprints. "

Ellen agreed. "Someone with Hinnenburg's credentials would have access to all of Los Angeles finest establishments. Many of the donors on his list were scientist, doctors and engineers. That film could contain any amount of valuable secrets."

Carson grinned wildly.

"Not anymore, Miss Patrick. My x-ray machine threw enough radiation to erase all of the contents of those canisters. Whatever information they may have contained is lost now."

O'Leary grumbled. "Guess that lets old Doc Hinnenburg off the hook. He'd have no reason to come back for useless documents."

"You're a genius!" Ellen proclaimed.

"I am?" The big dick uttered.

"Of course. If the whole scheme was based on getting this information out of the country, it makes sense that Hinnenburg would still want it. If he thinks the canisters still contain his micro-fiche, he'll stop at nothing to get them back."

Carson nodded. "You're going to lay a trap."

Ellen shook her head.

"Not me, the Domino Lady will, and I know just the person to help her!"

It was well past midnight when Detective O'Leary dropped Ellen Patrick back at the Roosevelt hotel. The burly Irishman had arranged for one of the uniformed patrolmen to fetch the car Ellen had borrowed from Jimmy. She took time to fetch a hundred dollar bill. She left the greenback in the glove compartment with a business card that read:

Compliments of the Domino Lady

She knew the buxom young nymph and her cheating boyfriend would never report the car missing. The dough would aid their deception further. Ellen had no qualms about that.

She would reward young Jimmy, the porter, handsomely upon her departure. Right now she wanted to get some sleep. She stripped off all her clothing and climbed into bed naked. She preferred to sleep that way.

Ellen rested her head comfortably. If her plans came to fruition, the case would be solved tomorrow. With a sigh of confidence, she closed her eyes and wandered off to slumber-land.

The next morning, Ellen Patrick was awoken by a tremendous rapping on her door. She clutched at the bed sheets.

"Miss Ellen? It be Jimmy. I got your daily."

Ellen raced from the bed quicker than usual. She haphazardly tied a bathrobe around her body. She kicked the bloody Domino Lady dress behind the chair.

"Good morning Jimmy."

The young porter was especially chippy this morning. He had noticed the car was returned, safe and unmarked.

"You sure do make the papers a lot." He blurted.

Ellen snatched the folded newspaper and studied the headline.

Moe Bernstein had relented his quest to bury the story of Franz Hinnenburg. Instead, he had placed it on page one with a huge headline that read:

Deception!

Bernstein had penned the tale himself.

The article mentioned how LAPD detective William O'Leary had uncovered a fraudulent plot to murder an innocent victim and disguise his corpse as that of Doctor Franz Hinnenburg. Bernstein didn't leave out any of the sordid details, including the cyanide suicides of the German accomplices, the charred remains of the unknown victim, and the intentions of the Germans to escalate anti-American protests in Berlin. Ellen already knew all that.

She scanned further down to the meat of the article where-in Bernstein proclaimed the discovery of the hidden micro-fiche. The story went on to explain that Ellen Patrick would give a press conference at noon to expose the true intent of the German's plot, including the contents of the micro-film.

Satisfied, Ellen tossed the paper.

"You look happier than a blue bird!" Jimmy announced.

"I am Jimmy. " She strolled over to her dresser and produced a sealed envelope. "This is for you, Jimmy. I've truly enjoyed my stay, but I'll be checking out this morning. Do me a favor, and make sure you spread the word that I'm leaving right after breakfast. Can you do that for me, Jimmy?"

The porter flashed his pearly whites.

"Shucks. I'd do anything for you, Ellen."

She caught the slip. Intended or not. It brought a sense of satisfaction to her mind.

"Good for you, Jimmy." She thought.

"Thanks again, Miss. I hope you enjoyed your stay."

"I did, Jimmy. And remember, make sure you blat that news out loud in the lobby, the dining area; anywhere you see a pair of ears. I need everyone to know I won't be occupying this room anymore."

Jimmy nodded, pretending to understand her odd command. He chalked it up to the notions of the rich and famous. He didn't bother to open her envelope. Whatever was in there would be a gift for his mother. Grinning, he departed, slamming the door.

Ellen didn't waste any time. She lined up the empty canisters she had retrieved from the corpse and laid them on the desk. Satisfied with the arrangement, she dropped her robe and picked out an outfit for the day, something flashy enough to show some leg, but long enough to conceal a weapon.

She settled on another colorful sundress, and after applying her make-up, she banged on the room wall three times before departing the room. If she were to encounter action, it would be best not on an empty stomach.

Ellen Patrick was greeted by a multitude of reporters when she made her entrance to the lobby. Photographers snapped pictures in a mad dash to get a close-up. Ellen noticed Mike Donovan heaving elbows in the crowd. She winked at him. The big man ran a hand through his mutton chops.

"Good morning. Miss Patrick!"

Ellen shook his hand. The other lensmen were incensed at the favoritism. She couldn't hear him over the din of the crowd so she pulled him tighter.

"If you want a scoop, leave this crowd and scope out my room." She whispered.

Donovan was smart enough to act natural. He ignored her statement, and asked about his colleague, James Evans. Ellen assured him that Doctor Carson was the most capable man for the job. Jim Evans would be back in the field shortly. For now, he deserved to enjoy bedside treatment with the beautiful candy-stripers and immaculately dressed nurses.

Ellen found herself jealous. She liked the feeling. Jim Evans had struck a chord with her. She planned on visiting the stricken photographer after this mess was resolved.

She continued to make her way through the crowd and past the front desk. Jimmy, the Porter, waved at her. She ran over and hugged him, much to the consternation of the watchful concierge. The rude gentleman simply pointed at his watch as he glared at Jimmy.

"Don't worry about him, Miss Ellen. I got bigger plans than carrying other people's bags all day. My mom thinks I should be a doctor. Ain't that something? A colored doctor. Boy that would be something."

Ellen released her grip.

"Jimmy, I don't ever want to hear that talk. A doctor is a doctor, regardless of skin pigmentation. You have every right to seek that goal.

Tomorrow, I want you to go down to County General and ask for Doctor David Carson. I'll tell him to expect you."

Jimmy squinted. "But I'm working tomorrow."

Ellen noticed the boy's eyes were locked on the concierge.

"Don't worry about that lout. I know the owners. He won't hassle you anymore. Just do as I ask and see Doctor Carson."

The boy nodded in agreement.

"Okay, Miss Ellen. And I did what you asked. I spread the word everywhere that you was checking out."

Ellen winked at him.

"Next time I see you, you better be in scrubs!"

Jimmy smiled back as he escorted her to a private dining table.

As Ellen dined on scrambled eggs and toast, a nefarious figure was fumbling with the lock on her door. Unbeknownst to the black clad figure, Mike Donovan was hunched on his hind legs underneath a table cloth that was covering a hallway phone. Donovan was snapping photos as quietly as possible.

With a minimal amount of effort, the tall masked figure shouldered his way into the hotel room. Mike Donovan lost sight of him. If he had been in there, he would have seen the intruder practically jump for joy at the sight of the canisters lined up on Ellen's desk. He withdrew a small duffle bag, and shoveled the canisters into it.

As this was taking place inside the room, Mike Donovan noticed the door to the adjoining room opening slowly. He recognized the figure that emerged. It was the hulking form of William O'Leary, the detective whose mug had been sprayed all over the morning edition of the Daily.

O'Leary was tip-toeing toward Ellen Patrick's room, service revolver in hand. Unfortunately, most of the hotel patrons were either sleeping or at breakfast so the hallway was unusually quiet. Donovan could hear the creaking of the big man's soles.

The intruder also had keen hearing. He wheeled just in time to see the big Irishman lunge at him. O'Leary had his revolver out, ready to whack the thug across the head, but the tall man was too fast. The blow merely glanced across his shoulder and he was able to absorb the impact.

"Halt, police!" O'Leary's booming voice commanded.

The masked man reacted instantly, swinging the duffle bag wildly at the detective. O'Leary was tired from being up all-night. His reflexes were a tad slow to avoid the hurling object. He felt his gun tangle up with the fabric of the bag.

"Confound it man. Don't make this tougher on you!"

The masked man ignored this advice. He reared back and clobbered Billy O'Leary with a series of overhand punches that pummeled the weary cop back into the hallway.

Mike Donovan continued shooting photos before embarrassment set in. He dropped his camera and raced in to assist the flailing detective. Unfortunately, his actions only hastened O'Leary's defeat. The burly Irishman staggered back, tripping over the photographer's feet. Both men tumbled to the ground.

As this took place, the masked intruder gathered up his duffle bag and fled toward the stairway. Freedom was only steps away. Laughing madly, he tore off the mask. It impaired his vision. This action revealed the well-known features of Doctor Franz Hinnenburg.

With the micro-fiche back in his possession, all the mad doctor had to do was lay low until he could hire a private jet or boat out of the country. Within the bag lay enough military and scientific secrets to destroy all of North America!

Hinnenburg raced down the winding stairway, his adrenaline flowing. He felt a resurgence of energy the closer he got to the exit. One of his spies had informed him earlier about Moe Bernstein's article. The doctor felt he was forced to act. Surely, a young woman such as Ellen Patrick would prove no obstacle in his quest to regain the intelligence stored inside those canisters. He hadn't counted on William O'Leary stumbling upon his entry, but he had dispatched him with ease. All that remained was eluding capture before his escape.

His heart beat faster as he spotted the door leading to the garage. He would take that route, the lobby off limits for obvious reasons. Just as he was about to plunge into the daylight, Hinnenburg saw a porter enter through the garage door.

It was Jimmy, returning from a smoke break. The young man smiled politely and held the door open. "Good morning, sir. May I help you retrieve your vehicle?"

Hinnenburg brushed by the youth, almost knocking him over in the process.

"Out of my way you inferior creature!"

Jimmy shifted out of the path casually. His actions were so nonchalant, the doctor eased up his speedy flight. It took him by complete surprise when Jimmy pitched a loud two fingered whistle in his direction.

"You foul thing! What kind of civilized manor employs your type?"

"I do." A voice echoed from the shadows of the garage.

The Domino Lady emerged, .22 automatic in hand.

Hinnenburg's eyes bulged, but only for a moment before producing his own weapon, a German Luger. He yanked Jimmy by the arm and placed the gun across the boy's temple.

"Drop that gun, girl, or I splatter this man's brains out."

Domino Lady moved closer, her automatic aimed at Hinnenburg's forehead. She was sure she could hit him from that distance, but she feared his reflexes might pull the trigger and kill Jimmy.

"I can't do that Hinnenburg. The world needs to know what you had planned."

Hinnenburg gripped the porter tighter.

"It was a glorious plan. The motherland approved it, and I set it in motion. We would disgrace you American swine, while at the same time incite an uprising among our proud people."

Domino Lady maintained her standoff.

"If you hurt the boy I will kill you."

Hinnenburg laughed. "Why do you care about this servant? He waits on your people's every needs. He can be replaced like any useful pet."

"I ain't nobody's servant!"

Jimmy, the Porter, slammed his head backward, staggering the towering German. The impact was enough to shake his grip and allow the youth to run free. Hinnenburg regained his bearing and leveled his gun at Jimmy's backside.

"Die dog!" He shouted, his finger clutching the trigger.

Jimmy closed his eyes. Thoughts of his mother filled his mind.

At that precise moment, Domino Lady fired her automatic, striking the German doctor in the throat. The big man grabbed at his neck as his legs wobbled, causing him to sink to his knees. He dropped the gun. Jimmy immediately swiped at it, sending the Luger under a parked car.

Domino Lady holstered her smoking weapon. She reached into Hinnenburg's duffle bag and pulled out a canister.

"There's nothing on this microfilm... you will die for nothing. O'Leary and I phoned Moe Bernstein last night and had him plant that story in this morning's paper. He was all too happy to oblige. I knew you'd take the bait. As soon as I was sure you were in the hotel, I exited the dining area through a bathroom window and donned my costume."

Hinnenburg watched as she removed the domino mask. His last earthly view was of the heavenly face of Ellen Patrick. She made sure Jimmy was out of sight.

"Ellen Patrick." The words dripped off his tongue. "You're the Domino Lady."

Ellen watched as he took his last breath. She reached into a sewn pocket in her costume and grabbed another business card. She draped it across Franz Hinnenburg's blood soaked shirt.

Compliments of the Domino Lady

Much to her surprise, Jimmy had fetched the same car from the night before.

"Thought you might be needing this," he suggested.

Domino Lady smiled securing her domino mask before he could get a glimpse of her face.

"Thank you. I have a friend to visit in County General."

Jimmy held the door open for her.

"Mind if I tag along for the ride?"

The Domino Lady nodded her approval. She knew William O'Leary and Mike Donovan could sort out the details with the feds. Her work here was done. It was time for Ellen Patrick to resume her life. She had some photographs to return to James Evans and an Olympic games to prepare for.

The End

AFTER THOUGHTS

I wrote Murder Games based on my fascination of the 1936 summer Olympic games. It was a fragile time for the entire world and the United States and her allies would soon be thrust into World War II. Espionage was carefully played out as countries were forced to make history altering decisions. The Domino Lady seemed a natural selection as her background and athletic ability lent itself to the tale.

ROBERT M. RICCI—was born and raised in Boston, Massachusetts, where he still resides. He grew up on a steady diet of pulp novels, comic books and reruns of 1960s TV series. His favorite pulp character is Doc Savage. Robert has written several other stories that have or soon will be featured in other Airship 27 Productions titles. Watch for them!

The Domino Lady
& the Spy Squad

Kevin Findley

As the distinguished looking, older man fell to the floor, the young woman with him grabbed a velvet bag from the dressing table and quickly left. She slowed at the top of the stairs, raised the hood of her black cloak and then went down overly careful as if she had celebrated this holiday too hard already.

At the bottom, she placed her hand with the bag behind her back and used her right hand to flip the cloak off of her shoulders. The quick movements revealed a stunning, white evening gown that covered an equally stunning body in its youthful prime. She crossed the foyer and approached a man she recognized who had just entered the front door to join the costume party.

"You're very late darling. Another few minutes and there will be no one left to kiss." As the confused, young man tried to figure out who the beauty was in the cloak and mask that circled him, he never felt her hand drop into his coat pocket and take his keys.

"Get me a drink Jason and I'll meet you in the ballroom. Then we can discuss why you're so late."

"Absolutely ... Gwen?"

She wagged her finger at him. "Close enough for a kiss Jason, but you'll have to do better than that for what comes after the kiss."

"See you in the ballroom doll!" With that he almost ran for the bar. Once Jason was out of sight, she moved just as rapidly out the front door and into the courtyard. As she had hoped, the confused young man's car was near the end of the driveway and not blocked in yet.

The lithe, young woman couldn't help but laugh while she threw her stolen car into gear and raced away from her victim's home and party. As she cleared the trees lining the driveway, the moonlight revealed her looking back over her right shoulder at the house. The hood had fallen back and her blonde hair was flowing around her. With no pursuit in sight, she opened the velvet bag on the seat next to her and lifted out the pearl and jade necklace to look at it again.

"I wish I could see you try to explain to your wife how you lost this pretty, little number Judge!"

The necklace went back into the bag with the other jewelry as well as a half empty syringe used to render the very amorous (and very crooked) Judge Herman Killabrew unconscious. Whoever found him would also find an open safe and an empty jewelry box on the bed. Carefully centered inside the box was a black and white calling card that read ... "Compliments of the Domino Lady"!

The masked thief and vigilante checked the dash clock in the Cabriolet and realized it was still only 11:50pm on New Year's Eve. There was plenty of time to make an appearance at the second costume ball held by Everett Linder, the equally crooked Chief of Health Inspections for Long Beach. His much younger wife was known to have a lovely collection of tennis bracelets to go along with her collection of tennis instructors.

"Let's see what pretty things you have waiting for me tonight Everett!"

Wakened by the ringing at her ear, Ellen Patrick quickly lifted her bed-side phone from its cradle and looked at the Tiffany clock; 4:16am. The calendar next to it showed her it was now January 15th, 1938.

"Hello?"

"Ellen, it's Roger McKane. I need to see you."

Typical man. "Sorry Roge; I'm glad you're in town, but I need my beauty sleep. Come by for brunch around 10:30 after I've put my face on."

"Thanks for the invitation Ellen but that isn't why I'm coming to L.A. I have to see you and your masked playmate."

Ellen smiled and instantly came fully awake. Anytime Roger McKane, Ellen Patrick's favorite private detective, wanted to see her alter-ego, it meant a bad time for crooks and a wonderful time for the Domino Lady.

"I'm not sure I can reach her today Roge. There's a phone number where I can leave her a message to meet us if she can. Now, tell me what this is all about."

"Do you recall the name Harry Raymond? He used to be a cop in L.A. and now he's a private detective."

Ellen paused, her delicate eyebrows knitted together. "I recall the name Roge but nothing else I'm afraid."

"Check the Times early edition for the details. You may get it before I arrive. Someone tried to blow up Harry in his own garage at Silverlake yesterday."

"Get here as soon as you can darling and tell me all about it."

"I'm close by. I'll get there be there in twenty minutes, Ellen."

The newspaper arrived less than ten minutes before Roger did. Ellen had just finished the article when the tall detective walked into the breakfast nook off the kitchen. She rose immediately and moved to embrace her former boyfriend and occasional ally.

Once she stepped back, Ellen reached up and tousled his brown hair. "You took longer to get here than I thought you would; I was getting worried."

"I wasn't in L.A.; I called from a phone booth in Camarillo."

"Were you in San Francisco when you found out?"

"No, I was in King City tracking down a city councilman's runaway daughter. Turned out she was twenty-two years old and had just married a fine young man of Irish descent. Daddy has an issue with Catholics. I called my service to pass along the good news and they told me about Harry." He nodded toward the paper.

"Read it yet?"

"Yes. I'm embarrassed to say I had forgotten Mr. Raymond was our Police Chief in '33. How well do you know him?"

"Harry came back to Los Angeles in '36. I knew of him then, but only met him last year after he joined forces with this citizen's group called CIVIC to investigate Mayor Shaw. He hired me to investigate one of Police Chief Davis' former detectives, Tom Garrett. Garrett left L.A. for San Francisco last year and tried to make a name for himself."

"Tried?" Ellen asked.

"Garrett was putting the squeeze on several of the tourist agencies and some of the fishermen. He didn't have the support of the local organization, but he did have some muscle from one of the unions that have been trying to get onto the fishing boats. I had just gathered enough to drag him to the cops when he disappeared right before Christmas."

"If he vanished in San Francisco how could he be involved with the bombing?"

"Garrett was part of what the papers call the LAPD's 'Spy Squad'. It's run by a police Captain named Earl Kynette. One of Harry's operatives claimed he saw him here in L.A. on the Sixth. If he's back in Davis and Kynette's good graces, he'll know exactly who was involved."

Ellen's brow crinkled. "Isn't this the same group of police officers that tried to block Okies from coming in to California last year?"

McKane nodded. "It was 1936 Ellen but yes, it was the same group. Harry thought that Garrett had fallen out of Shaw's favor when he screwed up a payoff to a couple of city councilmen and a newspaper editor so the Spy Squad's wiretapping activities wouldn't be made public."

"This is exactly the kind of corruption my Father worried about. Why didn't Mayor Shaw simply have him killed?"

"Shaw's not a guy who throws away anything. I'd bet that he and Davis had Kynette bring Garrett back to L.A. to set the bomb himself. It would take the heat off the spy squad and they could also blame the first bombing on Garrett as well."

"So that means Davis gets to stay mayor with no consequences?" Ellen snapped.

"Whoa Ellen! I'm on your side."

The young woman stretched her hand out to Roger. "Sorry."

McKane leaned over the table and placed his hand over hers. "There's no need to apologize. I understand how important this is to you; just try not to bite my nose off."

Less than two years ago, Owen Patrick was murdered by criminals and the corrupt political system that protected them from law enforcement. It was this heinous act that led his daughter, Ellen, to adopt the identity of the Domino Lady to seek justice for her father and the people he had worked so hard to protect.

The smile returned to Ellen's face and then her sense of humor returned as well.

"Is there anywhere else I can bite?" she asked with practiced innocence.

"When we're done with this Ellen, I promise to give you a complete list with order of preference."

"Oh good; I just love a to-do-list!" She said with a naughty little smile. "Now tell me how you think the Domino Lady and I can help with all this."

"I need to make a few phone calls first; speak to a member of the CIVIC group and a couple of operatives that work for Harry." He gestured toward the library/study and the phone he knew was in there. "May I?"

"Go right ahead dear."

While he was occupied, Ellen called for Marion to clear the table and read over the article again. Harry Raymond had been the Chief of the LAPD for just three months when he was dismissed in favor of a more reliable, political appointee. Bringing down Mayor Shaw was much more than just a job for him. As she finished, McKane returned.

"Ok Ellen, we're set. There's a meeting being held Monday and the head of CIVIC is with Harry now and getting as updated as possible. We'll join them downtown."

"Where is it?"

"Have you been to the Natural History Museum lately?"

As they drove to the museum Monday morning, Roger explained to Ellen the reason for the location and what would be happening. The light rain forced them to put the top up in Ellen's Roadster. The detective wasn't staying with Ellen since he needed to help Clinton's security keep a twenty-four hour watch over Harry Raymond at the hospital. That was fine with Ellen; she still needed to set up a meeting to fence the jewelry from her New Year's Eve caper.

"Like you read in the paper, CIVIC stands for Citizen's Independent Vice Investigating Committee. It was approved by Mayor Shaw, believe it or not. There was a grand jury investigating corruption with his administration and Shaw thought allowing this group to be formed would be a good way to take the heat off. Unfortunately for him, the committee chairman has enough money to be incorruptible to the political and criminal machines. The committee has grown past what Shaw had hoped for and is probably the biggest reform group in Los Angeles now."

"That's Clifford Clinton of Clinton Cafeterias; right?"

McKane nodded. "That's him. This is actually the second bombing. The first was Clinton's home back in October; fortunately, no was killed or seriously injured. Davis claims to know nothing about it but Earl Kynette runs the Spy Squad and I have no doubt Davis knows every pie Kynette has his fingers in despite the face he shows to the public."

"I remember that. Didn't the police try to imply that Clinton did it himself?"

"That's what Harry told me, yes." Roger took a breath and pressed on. "Since the Spy Squad is keeping the group under observation, regular meetings are scheduled and made public so Clinton's people can keep an eye out for who may be watching them. They photograph them when they can and look for familiar faces around their homes and businesses. A smaller steering group meets at member's homes to try and avoid being observed."

"Are they all still threatened and harassed?"

"Since the bombing at Clinton's home, he's been left alone. It was never the LAPD as a whole after him anyway; just the Spy Squad. Most cops enjoy eating at his cafeterias around Los Angeles like everyone else. Other members of CIVIC though have had their homes ransacked and their phones tapped."

"Can't they simply cut the wires or tear them out?"

"Yes, but they get replaced just as quickly and with no warrant, there's no proof the cops are behind it. CIVIC now tries to do everything they can face to face."

As they approached the Museum, McKane pointed to their left. "Pull in here Ellen. Mr. Clinton has rented the lot as valet parking, but it's really in order to have private security watching over everyone's cars."

Since this was one of the public meetings, it started out like any other city organization function. The notes from the last meeting were read and then Mr. Clinton updated everyone on Harry Raymond's injuries and investigation. It all went quickly off the tracks after that.

"Calm down! Everyone's car is being watched so nothing is going to happen."

"What about tomorrow Clifford? Are you sending home a guard with each of us?"

"Of course I can't Baxter! You have an actual garage in your home; lock it up."

"What about those of us who don't?!" yelled someone else.

Ellen leaned over and whispered. "They're more concerned about getting hurt than getting rid of Shaw. I can't say as I blame them after listening to that list of Harry Raymond's injuries."

"I understand that everyone is scared." Clinton continued, "My wife and I were terrified when our home was bombed three months ago. After several days of discussion, we decided that I had to continue going after Shaw. When something like this happens, you have to stand up or run and hide. We all know we can't hide any longer, this city is depending on us!"

A few men and women got up and began to applaud. Clinton looked slightly embarrassed but realized that he had the momentum again and pushed ahead to get more of them back on his side. By the end of the meeting, he had enough supporters calmed down to keep the committee alive and still dedicated to bringing down Mayor Shaw and his cronies.

Throughout the meeting, McKane had kept an eye on Ellen. As they left the Museum, he asked the important question.

"What did you think of them Ellen?"

"I think they're never going to get anywhere without some help; only a few of them really understand what they're up against. Most of them mean well, but they seem to think people will just fall into their lap to get rid of the crooks and dirty politicians. The rest just want to play at reformer to get their name in the paper."

Ellen stopped suddenly and turned to look at McKane. "Of course, that's exactly what some people would say about me. That's why you brought me here isn't it? To see this and convince the Domino Lady to help them out."

Roger had the decency to try and look embarrassed. "I won't deny it. These do-gooders are never going to get these dirty cops to turn on each other or the city officials who own them. I told Harry Raymond that, but he wouldn't believe me. They have to get the dirt on the crooks they work with and flip them like a flophouse mattress." He took Ellen's elbow and started walking again.

"UGH! I won't be able to get that image out of my mind for a week Roge!"

"Sorry Ellen, but this is exactly why I had you and the Domino in mind on the drive down here. The two of you working together have a real talent for making roaches, especially the wealthy ones, scatter and that's the best time to stomp on 'em."

Ellen couldn't help but smile at the unusual compliment. "Flattery will get you almost everywhere darling. All right then, I guess we're going mattress flipping and cockroach stomping. Where do we start?"

"I already have a crook in mind but it may depend on you Ellen. Tell me, exactly how fast of a girl are you?"

Ellen wasn't sure whether to kiss McKane or slap him, so she played it safe and did both.

"So Roge, how did this 'Stony' Proctor get his name?"

"He likes to dump the people who cross him in abandoned stone quarries and then drop rocks on them to hide the bodies."

Ellen rolled her eyes. "Oh lovely. At least he doesn't make them dig their own grave."

McKane scoffed. "That's only in the movies and pulps Ellen. As many times as I've been in trouble, I never once held a shovel."

"So why choose Stony Proctor out of the other crooks?"

"He used to be married to the sister of an LAPD Sergeant. The guy was on Stony's pad since he was a beat cop until the divorce. This same police officer has connections to both Vice and the Spy Squad."

"So I'm guessing that Stony did not come out well in the divorce?"

"You could say that. The judge left him with the clothes on his back and not much else. Business-wise, Stony was moved to a different territory after he and his now former brother-in-law started fighting in front of a protected gambling joint. It wouldn't have been a problem, except that a newspaper photographer was down the street snapping pictures of an accident and caught them on film."

"That wasn't very discreet of them."

McKane nodded. "So now Stony has to rebuild his reputation and whatever scams he had on the side. That makes him our best bet to flip on the cops. We just need a handle on him to turn the crank. That's where Twisty comes in."

Ellen raised an eyebrow. "We're using Twisty to make Stony turn?"

McKane grinned like a little boy. "I didn't do it on purpose Ellen!"

"I swear Roger McKane you're a ten year old child wearing his father's suit. OK then, same question; why Twisty?"

"Ed 'Twisty' Turner is a medium sized shark in Stony Proctor's pond. He's just smart enough to be trusted with simple to almost difficult tasks, but not smart enough for Stony to worry about him as a potential rival. He's dedicated to his boss and his only distractions are a love for fast cars and the women who drive them."

"So Proctor uses him to handle and keep track of low-level payoffs to local law enforcement?"

"Exactly Ellen. Twisty keeps the beat cops out of his gambling halls, brothels and other businesses. Stony has different middlemen pay off the higher-ups."

The young woman sat back for a moment and thought about it.

"So that means the uniformed officers on the take know if something happens to them, the higher ups can make evidence disappear and intimidate witnesses if they have to. On the rare occasions they can't make it all go away, the patrolmen know there's always a judge in someone's pocket and they'll be taken care of in jail for however a short time that is and after their release."

McKane grinned at her. "Glad to see you got your money's worth at Berkeley. The idea is to isolate each level of graft and corruption so if Internal Affairs or the District Attorney do catch a few uniforms, they won't have any proof their Sergeants, Lieutenants and Captains have any knowledge of it. When the investigation is done, these same men can assign new officers already dedicated to keeping the status quo."

"That's a great idea to use against district attorneys and reformers Roger, but not against someone like the Domino Lady."

"Or you Ellen. Regardless of how little evidence there may be, all the two of you need is a man to distract and you've already proven those are easy to find. Twisty always has a couple of armed guys in his house unless he has a girl there. We put you in a fast car and he'll toss them out for the night in a heartbeat."

"All compliments are welcome Roge but where are we going to get the kind of car we need to stomp on this first cockroach."

"I've got a former client who used to race at the L.A. Municipal Speedway until it closed in '36. Rex isn't going to be thrilled to hand over his beloved racer but he owes me a big favor. It might be best if you put on some sunglasses and a hat; maybe keep your distance from Rex. He doesn't know you and there's no reason why he should link us together."

Ellen looked thoughtful for a moment. "Perhaps you're right Roge. Tell you what, I have this beautiful, auburn wig I've been dying to try out. Not even you would recognize me."

"Even better Ellen! Thank you."

"For what?"

"You usually argue with me when I try to keep you out of something like this."

Ellen waved her hand. "Oh don't be silly. You said we need this car to get to Twisty and I happen to agree."

The next day, they drove over to Rex Mays home. The professional driver tried one last time to let him come with them and to let him drive.

"Blast it Roger, you know I need that car for trial runs in just a few weeks. If you wreck it, I may not be able to qualify for Indy this year!"

"Everyone of these guys is going to go nuts if you show up Rex. Besides, if someone finds out you were racing at a track that's been shut down, isn't that going to get you tossed off the circuit for the next few weeks anyway?"

"That's better than getting my car wrecked on top of it!"

"I can absolutely promise you Rex; there is no way I'm going to do anything to wreck that car."

Mays nodded toward the disguised Ellen. "You're not going to let her drive are you?"

"Trust me Rex. I haven't given a single thought to letting her behind the wheel."

Still unhappy, Mays finally let Roger put the car on a trailer and mournfully let them leave. On the way home, Ellen was full of questions.

"Why won't you tell me what it was Roge?"

"What was what Ellen?"

"What did you do for Rex Mays that he let you take his car?"

"Client confidentiality darling; can't tell you."

Ellen put on her best pout. "Then maybe I'll go back and ask Rex myself."

"Ha! If he comes clean with you Ellen, I'll provide free detective services for the rest of your life!"

Now irritated, she pushed her sunglasses back up her nose, slid down in her seat and crossed her arms. "All those wonderful secrets and you won't tell me a single one. I'm beginning to think you don't like me anymore Mister McKane."

"That'll never happen and you know it Ellen. Now, at the risk of making you pout even further, has Domino called you back yet?"

"Oh! Didn't I tell you Roge? She was upstairs listening last night. She knows everything."

"Why you dirty, little sneak!"

"Ha!" Ellen wagged her fingers at Roger. "Drive on to the airport Mister McKane."

Ellen had rented a private airfield to store the car and because Roger wanted her to practice before he would give her the keys. When they arrived, it almost dinner time and the sun was beginning to set. Once Roger unhooked the trailer, they locked up the hangar and departed for the city.

"Now that the car is put away, are you going to start teaching me how to drive tomorrow?"

"Yes, but there's still time to change your mind Ellen. We can always follow Twisty from the racetrack to his house."

"I'll be fine Roge. All I have to do is keep Twisty distracted. With myself and Rex's car in his rear-view mirror, he won't be looking at anyone or anything else. He'll never know that Domino is following us. Like you said, the only time he doesn't have guards hanging around is when he's 'entertaining' a girl."

"Once you convince me you can handle Rex's car, that is."

"I am an excellent driver Roger McKane and you know it."

"We'll see about that."

"Drive on to the airport Mister McKane."

The next morning, Ellen allowed Roger to drag her out of bed with the sun.

"I know you can drive very fast on dry, paved roads in ideal conditions. However, this is a finely tuned racer that will go about thirty to forty miles per hour faster than your roadster on nearly every type of surface. If Rex knew you were driving, he never would have let me have the car, regardless of how big a favor he owes me."

"Fine, let's get started." She threw the car in gear and took off on the private airfield they had rented. It was two narrow airstrips connected at three points with dirt road access.

Ellen held the accelerator at 40 mph to the far end of the strip and then turned hard onto the access. She held the auto steady and then downshifted as the rear wheels touched pavement and turned left onto the second airstrip. In a few seconds, she had accelerated to 50 mph and executed the same maneuver.

"OK, Roge; let's show off a little bit."

She quickly accelerated to over 60 mph and perfectly crossed to the second airstrip again. Without missing a beat or a shift, Ellen increased her speed to 85 mph and then performed a perfect 'S' using all three access points; twice.

Ellen finished her demonstration by stepping on the brake hard and came to a halt with the driver's door directly in front of McKane. She killed the engine and then got out to look at Roger, who stared back at Ellen; mouth agape.

"I guess I'm ready for tomorrow night. Don't look so surprised Roge. When a man can only think of kissing a woman or running his fingers through her hair, he will tell or show her anything that she wants to know."

The tall detective nodded. "I can certainly attest to that. So who taught you how to drive and maneuver?"

She winked at McKane and shook her head. "Client confidentiality darling; can't tell you."

Roger could only stand there with his mouth open again while Ellen sashayed away like a metronome toward the hangar.

"That's why she didn't argue with me about the sunglasses and hanging back. She didn't want Mays to recognize her. Holy Moses, she's the one who stole Rex's car back in '36."

Despite the Los Angeles Speedway being officially closed, drivers still met at the airport track to race and show off new cars or how they customized their old ones. The airfield manager generally left them alone unless he thought things were getting out of hand and called the police. Even then, it was more likely the cops who arrived would spend the next few hours looking under hoods instead of arresting them.

It was still a great training ground for drivers getting started and old rum runners who missed getting chased by the police in their younger days. Twisty was the unofficial president of this crowd and was always on the lookout for fast cars and faster women. Ellen Patrick planned on being the fastest woman the thug had ever seen or ever would.

She pulled in close, threw the racer into neutral and then revved the engine.

"Hello boys and girls! Got room for one more?"

"With a ride like that darlin', you can park anywhere you want!"

Ellen parked as close to the center of the group as she could, got out and strolled over.

"Who are you and where can I get a racer like that?" For once, the young socialite found herself not to be the center of attention; at first.

"I'm Winnie and you need to have good friends that like to lend out their toys."

An older man, who never took his eyes off the car, asked; "Mind if we look under the hood?"

"Go right ahead!" Ellen began looking for anyone fitting Twisty's description. She found him leaning over a Packard, standing next to a brunette that was staring death back at Ellen.

"Watch out for Sandra there, if you don't know your engine inside and out, she may just take a swing at 'ya."

Ellen guessed that she was maybe three to five years older than herself. At first glance, the brunette was dressed like the others. Then Ellen noticed that Sandra wasn't wearing heels or canvas shoes, but lace-up, leather brogues like the ones she had on. Sandra also filled out her Capris nicely, but they weren't so tight as to restrict movement.

She was near enough a dark-haired mirror image of Ellen that the young socialite began to wonder just who she was. Then Sandra began walking toward her.

"You're only sore because I decked you one Dale ... and then I fixed your carburetor." The group roared and Dale could only shrug and rub his jaw. Although the banter stayed light in the group, Ellen noticed Sandra kept an eye on Twisty no matter where he went. Whoever she was, the tough looking mechanic thought she was the queen bee around here and Twisty was her favorite drone.

"Hey,Winnie! Where did you get a beauty like this? She's ready to go!"

Ellen turned back to Dale. "Like I said, you have to have good friends."

"Why don't you let me have a turn behind the wheel?" She turned to see Twisty had walked up behind her.

"Oh I don't think so. Rex made me promise that I wouldn't let anyone else drive her. I think he's hoping to go Indiana for some little race in a few months?"

"Rex? As in Rex Mays?"

"Oh you know Rexy?" The crowd around them grew quiet and moved in closer at hearing Rex Mays' name.

"You know him?" Twisty asked.

"He's a friend of the family; sort of."

One of the other drivers looked skeptical. "I don't recognize this car."

"I saw him race it in Florida last year." Another driver popped up.

"Well he did say that he used to race another car here before the track closed." Ellen responded.

Twisty looked like someone had just run off with his wife. "Yeah, this place was a sweet deal back then. Guys set records nearly every race and you could count on at least one crash every weekend to keep things interesting." The other drivers around him nodded solemnly like they were in church.

Ellen moved in a little closer and began flirting. "I didn't catch your name."

"Twisty."

"I'm Winnie. Nice to meet you." Ellen took Twisty's hand with a gentle grip and then slowly withdrew, stopping at his fingertips for a moment. The big thug nearly fell forward when she finally pulled away.

Ellen grinned and looked around the crowd. "Who here wants to have a little race?"

Sandra walked up to Ellen and stopped just before they would have bumped.

"Maybe you can drive, but if you don't have a few busted knuckles, you don't belong here Blondie. Go back to your studio or wherever else it is you like to pretend."

Ellen's return smile was an iceberg. "Maybe he'd rather be my Dagwood than your Pa Kettle." Then she shoved Sandra, hard.

I can't just put her down, Twisty might take her side out of sympathy. I'll take it easy on her at first and see what happens.

Sandra came back immediately; hands up like she just heard the referee say "Fight." Ellen barely dodged the first punch before she got her own hands up. The second one to her chin stopped her move forward cold. She barely stepped back in time from the third one that would have snapped her head around.

OK, enough of that. Let's see if she can take it.

Ellen took two more blows on her forearms and moved in again. She feinted with her right elbow at Sandra's chin and then locked the brunette's right wrist back with her left hand. She grabbed the elbow with her right and twisted the arm up and backwards, slamming Sandra into a Packard, stretching her across the hood. Ellen followed with a right to the stunned woman's temple and let her slide to the ground.

The blonde avenger took a step back and did a double-take when Sandra looked up, smiled and put out her hand for help. Ellen offered her own in return and pulled her up. Once she got on her feet, Sandra looked at Twisty and back to Ellen.

"OK," she said and held up her index finger, "you can have him once."

"Hey wait a minute!" Twisty points a thumb at his chest. "I'm the man and I decide who comes home with me."

Sandra walked up to Twisty and put a hand over his. "Men are awful cute when they're confused, aren't they Winnie?" Then she grabbed Twisty's chin and gave him a hard, long kiss.

She looked at Ellen again. "Remember, once." Then she got in her Coupe and sped away, covering everyone in dust.

Ellen looked at Twisty. "Well, you heard the woman."

Twisty walked toward his car with the look of a confused man heading for the electric chair. He looked back once to make sure Ellen was ready to go and then drove home.

Once they pulled up to Twisty's house, it took him two minutes to run everybody off. Ellen let him back under the hood of Mays' racer again and talked for about five minutes before she casually mentioned she was thirsty. As they walked inside, Twisty moved the conversation to her.

"I never saw a woman punch like that until I met Sandra a few months ago. She nearly spun Dale in a full circle. Now there's two of you."

"I've always gone after the biggest fish in the pond. No reason to change my ways now."

"Ha! You're talking like an old woman fighting for the best chair at Bingo." Suddenly a pleading tone entered his voice.

"Come on Winnie! You've got to introduce me to Rex Mays; I'll do anything for you."

"Mix me a drink big guy and then we can talk about meeting Rex. I need to freshen up." *Let's hope he falls for this.* The plan, as far as Roger knew, was to let Domino Lady in and they would take care of Twisty together. Then they would ransack the place for any information they could use against Stony. Ellen would just pretend to find her alter-ego, scream and wait for Twisty to come running.

BAM! BAM! BAM!

Ellen's heart jumped at the pounding on the front door. *I wonder if Sandra changed her mind.* She exited the bathroom quickly and returned to the living room to find Stony Proctor standing there.

"Who's the broad?"

"This is Winnie boss. That car you saw outside belongs to Rex Mays! She knows him personal like."

"Yeah that's real nice Twisty. We need to talk."

"I can wait outside if you want me to." Ellen pointed to the patio off the kitchen.

Stony shook his head. "Make tracks out the door doll. Twisty and I have a lot to talk about. You two can play in the garage some other time."

Ellen looked at Twisty. "How about it?"

"Can you meet me at the track next week?"

"Yes, but I may not have the car."

Twisty winked at her. "Bring Mays and we'll call it square Winnie."

Ellen left and drove to the nearest phone booth she could find. No answer at home, Roger had already left to watch over Harry Raymond. She returned the receiver and walked back to the car.

Stony said they had a lot to discuss. It's already getting late and I doubt he's going to call back his security. I can still do this!

Feeling the thrill of the chase once more, she turned the ignition, threw the car in gear and drove to the airfield as fast as the road would allow.

Once she had the racer back in the hangar, Ellen slid the door back in place and locked it. She avoided turning on the overhead lights and felt her way back to the roadster to turn on the dashboard lights.

Although she was prepared to deal with Twisty without her alter-ego (the syringe was in her purse), Ellen felt a certain relief as she opened the overnight case on the passenger seat. Until she had brought all of her Father's killers to justice, she wanted no one to associate her face and name with her vigilante activities and needed the anonymity the mask gave her.

Ellen removed her brogues and socks, then shed her jacket, blouse and Capris. She hooked a garter belt around her waist and quickly slipped on garters and silk stockings, then attached them to the belt. Removing the black cloak and white evening gown from the case, Ellen slipped the dress over her head and arms, then worked it down past her shoulders with a shrug; slowed momentarily at her chest. A twist of the hips sent the hem down to cover her shapely legs and stop just before touching the ground.

She checked her syringe and .22, placing them in a small bag that went into the glove compartment. The overnight case with the discarded clothing went into the trunk.

With everything else put away, the bombshell vigilante changed the license plate on her roadster.

Ellen felt the mask in its hidden pocket in the cloak and smiled. Then she swiftly moved the car out of the hangar, locked it and put on the mask.

The Domino Lady stepped on the accelerator and sped to Twisty's home.

She drove past the house to make certain everyone was gone and then turned around to park it several houses up. Moving quietly, she went around to the back, knowing the patio door would be the easiest way to break in.

Once through the door, the Domino Lady could hear voices and hesitated before stepping further inside. After a moment, she realized that it was Twisty talking to himself, slurring his words.

"Stupid Stony. Winnie's a great gal; she'd have to be to get Rex Mays to let her borrow his car. He wasn't even here a whole hour, she coulda waited on the patio fer cripes' sake! Stupid Stony."

Maybe this will be easy for once.

The masked woman carefully eased up behind Twisty and removed the syringe from her garter as she reached for his neck.

The big man suddenly sniffed the air and sat up.

"Winnie?"

Before he could turn around, the Domino Lady grabbed his left ear and turned his head hard. The syringe went in before Twisty could reach back and he was unconscious by the time she pulled the needle out.

"Chanel and motor oil. The thug's got a nose like a bloodhound."

Since Twisty was only the first roach to be stepped on, the Domino Lady didn't take any of the files she found in his desk. Instead, she photographed them using a Falcon Miniature. As she pulled the last of the files from the bottom desk drawer, she noticed a thin, metal cash box on the bottom.

Setting the papers aside, she lifted the box out and used a letter opener to break the lock. Inside were stacks of $10 and $20 bills with the bank wrappers still on them. The blonde beauty had just found a $1500 payday.

"Well, Roge never said I couldn't take home any loose change I found now did he?"

After she completed the photography, the bombshell vigilante returned the contents to their file drawer. She made it obvious that every drawer in the desk had been searched, moved every object on a flat surface and pulled all the paintings in the room off the walls in order to make it appear robbery was the only goal. Once that was finished, she left her calling card on top of the now empty cash box on Twisty's desk.

"Do you want to take this to the CIVIC people?"

Roger shook his head while he hung the last photo to be developed from the Domino Lady's efforts last night. "Not all of it Ellen. Much of it is low level pay-offs that would just waste their time right now." He pulled the blackout curtain he had rigged across the pictures and then he and Ellen stepped out of the large closet into the bathroom and then out into the main hallway."

"I don't know every one of these names, but I'll take every one that's a Sergeant or higher to Clinton's people. They may have names and photographs of some of the cops listed here. It would help to know what these guys look like."

"Let's check with Marion and see if she's got lunch laid out yet."

"That's one of the perks about working with you Ellen. Marion's cooking."

"The best one?"

"It's certainly in the top five." He said with a straight face.

Fifteen minutes later, they had finished lunch and laid out the pictures over the large desk in the study. Marion has been dismissed for the day and the gardener wouldn't be back until Monday. Roger pulled out a folder he got from CIVIC to compare notes and Ellen put her chin in her hands to think. After a few moments, she spoke.

"Other than knowing who to look for, the names really won't do the Domino, or us any good. She needs to know where to go next; specifically, she has to know where to hit Stony Proctor to not really hurt him, but to try and get more information that a District Attorney can use."

McKane smiled as Ellen spoke. As beautiful as she was, Roger recognized that the brain behind that pretty face was the more dangerous weapon. Between those and the family connections that gave her entry into high society throughout California, Ellen was a triple threat. *If I could convince her to join me in San Francisco, we'd be able to hang out our own shingle. Add in the Domino Lady as a 'silent partner' and no other agency could touch us.*

"So for us uneducated, private flatfoots, what you're saying is we need to climb higher up the food chain."

Ellen patted his hand, "And to think Daddy once believed you were simple. That's very good Roge."

McKane sighed and looked upward in search of support. "Oh why do I put up with you and that wicked sense of humor?"

"Play your cards right Mr. McKane and perhaps I'll remind you after this is over."

"That's what I'm hoping for Ellen, but first let's see if you can't identify a few lions in their den. If we can organize a meeting with Stony and you can drop the right names ..."

"It will push him in our direction." Ellen finished.

"Collect your kewpie doll beautiful!"

"So now I have to walk right in to the Spy Squad and spy on them. Sounds exciting!"

The simplest way for a socialite to get into a police station was to get caught someplace they shouldn't be and use their family name to get out before they made the blotter. Since Ellen wanted to identify as many police officers as possible, the next easiest way was to walk in the front door, file a report over some minor issue and then charm her way through as many departments as possible before getting thrown out as a very pretty, but not too bright, nuisance.

It made complete sense to use the bruise on her face and scratch under her chin to file a reckless driving report against the person who cut her off on the way home last night. Between that and the occasional tear, Ellen quickly found herself with access to nearly every office in the building and every police officer in them.

She finally made her way into the Spy Squad offices and was once again surrounded by detectives willing to give her anything from mug shot books to a ride home; not necessarily hers of course. After five minutes, Capt Earl Kynette and his right hand, Lieutenant Elmo Wahl noticed the growing crowd.

"Excuse me Miss. Are these flatfoots bothering you?"

"Oh I'm fine Lieutenant ....?"

"It's Kynette, Captain Kynette."

"Oops, I'm sorry!"

"That's quite all right Miss. What is your business with the LAPD today?"

"Oh, I've been helped!" She showed Kynette the report she had filled out. "I was told to take this to an office on the fourth floor, but I guess I've gotten off the elevator on the wrong one." Noticing how hard Kynette was looking at her, *I also need to get out of here before I use up my luck for the year.*

He looked at the report for a moment. "That's all right Miss Patrick. All you have to do is go out that door, turn left and take the stairs down two flights." Kynette was smiling like a benign grandfather, but his eyes made him look like a mountain lion that just spotted a rabbit.

"Thank you so much." Ellen squeezed his arm and quickly departed.

Kynette turned to Wahl and the smile dropped instantly. "The name and face look familiar. Find out who Miss Patrick is and if I have another problem to deal with." Then he went into his office.

The Lieutenant waved at another detective. "Elliot! Follow that blonde out and see what car she gets into. Then call in to our boy over at DMV and get a cycle cop to pull her over. Have him find out where she's going and then call back to my extension."

"What if it's a cab?"

"Then have him pull the driver over to check his hack license and ask her anyway."

"Anything else Elmo?"

"Have a couple of guys check out where she lives. Make it careful, don't ransack the place."

"You sure about this? She looks like any other rich girl who wants to go slumming downtown without getting too dirty."

Wahl looked around and lowered his voice. "We're not taking any chances since the deal on Harry Raymond didn't come out like we wanted." The stocky cop thought about it for a moment. "Put Garrett on this. Tell him if he can't search a house properly then he better run back to his fishermen and tour guides."

Twenty minutes later Elliott Necker walked up to Wahl's desk.

"You aren't going to like this Elmo. That broad is Owen Patrick's daughter."

"Elliott, you better be pulling my leg."

"Nope, to make it worse, our surveillance team watching CIVIC saw her at a meeting with Clinton."

Wahl swore and pushed himself back from the desk. Since CIVIC was the biggest thorn in Mayor Shaw's side right now, that made the group one of his biggest headaches. He motioned Necker to follow him. They walked two flights up to the roof. The senior policeman lit a cigarette and shook one out for the sergeant.

"This isn't good. Owen Patrick went after the State government and crooked businessmen for the most part. Davis never thought of him as a threat to us and Shaw knew that he'd be the first guy blamed if anything ever happened to the guy."

"Why's that if Patrick wasn't a problem?"

"The two of 'em had a run-in before Shaw became Mayor. Don't know the details, but apparently he embarrassed Shaw pretty good in front of the hoi polloi he was trying to raise money from for his campaign."

"Do you think someone at CIVIC put his daughter onto us?"

"Maybe. Find out if she's been playing do-gooder for awhile or if this is something new." He looked at Necker and flipped his cigarette butt away. "You got any other good news for me?"

"There was a guy she was with at the CIVIC meeting. One of our guys recognized him, but can't put a name on him."

"Did he get a picture?"

"Yes, we're running it around the building now."

Wahl almost lit another cigarette but put it back in the pack. "Is Patrick still living in that pile of bricks her father left her?"

"It's listed as the primary residence; Garrett's on the way now. There's also an apartment in Long Beach."

"Get someone else out there too; same procedure, search it, don't wreck it."

"Why Officer, was I really going too fast?" Ellen pulled down her sun-glasses and put on her best little girl pout. The young Highway Patrol Officer actually fell back a step and took a moment before he could speak again.

"Yes Ma'am, err Miss, you were traveling at sixty miles per hour when I pulled you over. The limit for this section of the highway is fifty."

"I am sooo sorry Officer."

"May I see your license and registration please?"

"Of course!"

Instead of leaning sideways, Ellen turned and leaned over the shift to open the glove compartment. Patrolman Coughlin found himself so en-tranced by the view that when Ellen turned back around, he fumbled and nearly dropped his ticket book onto the asphalt.

"I'm not sure which one is the registration. Would you mind too much looking for me please?" She handed him every paper that was in the glove compartment.

"I'll still need your license as well."

"Oh it should be in there too. The gardener got tired of having to bring it to me because I always forget to move it when I change purses."

"Why's that if Patrick wasn't a problem?"

Poor little rich girl, wonderful.

"Let's see; restaurant receipt, gas receipt, Lena's House of Lingerie, ..."

Ellen squealed and grabbed, "I'm so glad you found that! Would you believe that brassiere didn't even fit and the mean little salesgirl refused to believe me? Humph! Like that flat-chested little so-and-so would ever have use for one in the first place." She waved the receipt. "Now I'll get my money back!"

"Ummm, ahhh, glad to help." Coughlin began to hand Ellen back her papers and then realized he hadn't looked at anything yet. He found her registration, checked it against her license and then looked at Ellen again.

"Where are you going in such a hurry Miss Patrick?"

"Oh I'm just heading home. I spent the day downtown and now I want to go swim away the dirt and sweat."

"That sounds like a very nice idea Miss Patrick. Just please slow down and try get there in one piece."

Ellen turned her smile up to almost blinding. "It's so nice to know that someone cares about little old me Officer Coughlin." She grabbed the papers from him and tossed them back into the glove compartment, making sure to give him another view.

"Thank you for not giving me a ticket!" Then she turned the ignition and drove off before he could say anything.

The now very smitten uniformed officer went back to his motorcycle, executed a U-turn and stopped at the first gas station. He pulled up next to the phone booth outside, dismounted and dialed the operator.

"This is Patrolman Sean Coughlin, badge number 8832. Patch me through to LAPD Headquarters, extension 614."

"Standby." replied the operator. In thirty seconds, connections were completed and Wahl's voice came through.

"You found the broad Sean?"

"Yes Lieutenant. It was pretty easy to spot that little, red roadster of hers."

"Did you find out where she's headed?"

"She said she was going home."

"That should be OK. Our boys will have plenty of time to check out that pile of bricks she lives in up in the hills before she gets there."

"Are you sure about this Lieutenant? She's pretty enough, but I don't think her elevator goes all the way up."

Wahl gave a sharp laugh, "All the better for her Sean. If there's any evidence she's involved with the New Year's society robberies, we'll have to make sure Ellen Patrick spends her weekends in Lompoc and not on the beach."

"Understood, Lieutenant. Do you have anything else for me?"

"That's it for today Coughlin. Just finish out your shift. Say, you didn't give her a ticket did you? I don't want any paper on this stop."

"Of course not, Sir."

"Good!" Wahl hung up without another word. He put his meaty hands behind his head and leaned back in his chair. *Coughlin's a good tool, but he's too honest for me to use on the Squad. Ellen Patrick's probably nothing, just a slumming socialite like Elliott thinks. Still, she is Owen Patrick's daughter. If she pops up again, I'll have to tap her phones.*

Unknown to Wahl, Officer Coughlin had the perpetrator of the New Year's society robberies right in front of him. Since they were private homes of "connected" people, there was no official police report filed and the press was still unaware that these men had been robbed, let alone by the Domino Lady.

Ellen watched the motorcycle cop in her rear view mirror as he crossed the median and departed away from her. *If he wanted to convince me I was speeding, he should have waited longer than thirty seconds after I passed a limit sign. Too bad, he is rather cute on that bike!*

The young woman pushed down the accelerator and grinned. *Let's see if another one can catch me before I stop for lunch!*

Finding no one at home, Garrett and another plainclothes officer picked the lock on the kitchen door and went into the house. After looking around downstairs for a moment, the detective started giving orders.

"Mike, you check the upstairs. I'll start with this library and then join you."

Garrett went in and began checking behind pictures. With no safe found, he began searching behind the larger books on the shelves. After several minutes, he discovered one behind a shelf of oversized map books.

"What the ...?!" The safe came open at a turn of the handle. Nothing inside.

Heading upstairs, the crooked cop began with Ellen's room. He picked up a picture of Ellen taken with her Father at her graduation from Berkeley and looked it over.

"She's a babe, that's for certain. Educated too? It sure pays to be a pampered, rich girl." He put the picture carefully back where it had been.

Moving to the walk-in closet, Garrett found a white, evening gown hanging next to a black cloak. He whistled appreciatively.

"I'll bet she looks like Carole Lombard in that dress."

He opened the jewelry box and got stunned for the second time. Garrett didn't know a lot about jewelry, but the pearl and jade necklace he held would have stood out even to a guy who had never bought anything outside a Tiffany's. He poked around the jewelry box for another moment and then carefully put the necklace back.

"How many tennis bracelets does one broad need anyway?"

Mike walked in. "Garrett. I found a safe in the master bedroom, but you're not going to believe this."

Tom shook his head. "It's unlocked and empty."

"How'd you know?"

"Same thing for the one downstairs and in here."

"This dame is screwy Tom. That master bedroom is dusted, but it looks like no one has been there in over a year."

"That's got to be her father's room."

They went back downstairs and searched the kitchen and laundry rooms.

"Tom, look at this." He showed the senior policeman two brown bottles.

"What have you got?"

"Developing fluid. I didn't see any boxes of pictures upstairs. Did you see anything downstairs?"

"No. Hey, go see if you smell anything in the bathrooms."

It only took a moment for Mike to return.

"I caught a whiff in the WC just off the study. Someone was developing pictures yesterday, day before at most."

Garrett looked at his watch. "Run through the bedrooms one more time. I'll check the study again and then keep lookout in case Patrick returns. If I miss her, go out one of those lanai doors."

"That's it Lieutenant. We got out of there before Patrick returned home. There was no one in the car with her, but she sure took her time getting back."

"The guy she was with at Clinton's meeting was Roger McKane, the snooper that was trailing you in San Francisco. You see any sign of him?"

Garrett nearly snarled. "No, but if I find him, I'll fix him myself."

"Like you tried to fix Harry Raymond?"

"Next time, let me get up close and not plant a bomb! I told you and Kynette both it was a lousy idea. If Raymond's wife had been in the car, Davis would have found a shovel big enough to bury all three of us and you know it!"

"Yeah, you may be right about that." Unconsciously, Wahl rubbed the back of his neck. "OK, it looks like Ellen Patrick is just another run of the mill do-gooder. Get back in here tomorrow and catch up on what else is happening."

Ellen walked into her home and immediately noticed that something was different. Although Roger McKane smoked cigarettes, he did it outside at Ellen's request. The stale cigar she smelled was certainly not his.

"Marion, has anyone been in the house recently besides you, myself and Mister McKane? Did you accept a delivery or did the gardener return for something?"

"I received no packages Miss Patrick. Donald finished his duties yesterday and said he won't need to return until Monday."

"Have you been here most of the day?"

"No, I arrived shortly before noon. I'm sorry, was I supposed to be here earlier?"

"Of course not Marion. I'm probably just being silly. Go ahead and finish up for the day." The housekeeper departed to finish the week's laundry.

Ellen thought for a moment, then hurried upstairs. She checked the jewelry taken on New Year's Eve to find it was all still there. The items in the jewelry box had been moved though. A cold chill ran down her spine and she went downstairs to speak to Marion again.

"Would you take a box home with you tonight and keep it for a few days please?"

"Of course Miss Patrick."

"Thank you Marion. I'll have it ready for you when you go home tonight."

The next day, Ellen and Roger attended another CIVIC meeting. She decided not to tell him of her suspicions since he would ask why the Domino Lady would keep her stolen gems in Ellen's closet. Once he did, it would only be a matter of minutes before he figured out her secret.

This time, they stepped out from the main meeting and discussed the pictures taken with Clifford Clinton and a smaller group. Although the restaurateur trusted Roger due to his connection with Harry Raymond, he was very unhappy with the private detective bringing Ellen and the Domino Lady into their affairs.

"This committee has to present a package of evidence to the District Attorney that is beyond reproach. If it doesn't, then Shaw and his minions will walk away scot-free like they always do."

As they prepared to leave, one of the people from the main meeting moved quickly to intercept them. Dark-haired, well-dressed and poised, she appeared only a bit older than Ellen herself. When she moved directly in front of Ellen though, the blonde socialite could see the other woman was over thirty and despite the expertly applied make-up, she had not lived like this for very long.

"Hello Ellen. My name is Catherine Edwards."

"Oh yes, you married Anson Edwards last Thanksgiving." *At a quickie ceremony in Mexico just after his wife died.* Ellen thought but didn't say.

"Yes; would you have a few minutes to speak privately?"

McKane jumped in, "Can you tell us what this is about?"

Catherine looked at Ellen who nodded. "I may have some information about Mayor Shaw and how it relates to the death of Ellen's Father."

Once they were seated and the waiter departed with their orders, Catherine spoke up first.

"I suggest we don't waste each other's time. You know my history Ellen; in fact everyone knows how and where Anson and I met. Even Edith knew before she died. I can't say she gave me her blessing, but she didn't hate me either."

"I find that difficult to believe Catherine."

"Really, Ellen? You've met Anson's sons. How long do you think Charles and Calvin would have waited to force Anson out of the house if he didn't have an ally living there with him? If cancer hadn't taken Edith, she would have died from the heartbreak those two were causing her."

"All right, I'll grant you that. Now what does this have to do with my Father? He was killed almost a year before you married Anson."

"The 'house' where I met my husband is protected by the LAPD Vice Squad. It's not raided for a percentage of the weekly proceeds and what you might call reasonable visitation privileges by senior police officers."

The older woman hesitated and then continued. "The week before your Father died, Lieutenant Elmo Wahl and one of his men paid us such a visit. The sitting room they were in used to have a fireplace in it. The chimney is walled up now, but if you stand in an alcove in the room upstairs, you can still hear what is being said below."

Their order arrived and the conversation stopped for a moment. Catherine's hand shook slightly as she stirred cream into her coffee.

"Before their companions for the evening arrived, they were discussing what to do with a local figure. Wahl said that 'Shaw wants that damn lawyer quiet. Either pay him off or shut him up permanently.' This was just three days before Owen Patrick was killed."

Ellen maintained her composure, but Roger recognized the flash of anger in her eyes.

"How certain are you Catherine? Did you hear this yourself?"

"Yes, I heard Wahl say that to the other policeman, Mr. McKane." She turned her head to look at Ellen directly.

"I know this is a lot for you to take in Ellen. I wish I had come forward after your Father's death, but I was just too scared for so long. When I saw you again at the meeting tonight, I couldn't keep quiet any longer."

"It's all right Catherine. I've always known that the corruption my Father sought to expose went high, but to have my suspicions confirmed is still ... unsettling."

"Are you OK Ellen?"

"Not yet Roge, but I will be. I just need to see a man about a fence."

Garrett looked at the photographs of Mrs. Killabrew's jewelry. He instantly recognized the pearl and jade necklace from Ellen Patrick's bedroom.

"Is this everything that was taken from the Judge?"

"No, there were also a couple of watches that he hadn't photographed." Necker looked up. "Do you recognize something?"

"The necklace is familiar, but maybe I saw it on the Judge's wife. I worked security for them a couple of times when I was still in uniform. Do you have anything from the Linder robbery Elliot?"

"No photographs, just a list of what was taken."

Garrett looked at the list without really seeing anything; his mind was making the connections. "Judge Killabrew admitted it was that Domino Lady broad?"

Necker laughed. "He did to us. He told his wife it was a masked intruder that knocked him over the head. Fortunately she didn't find him 'cause he was snoring like a band saw."

"I don't see a Robbery report. Has anyone checked with them yet?"

"Not officially, Wahl's got a beef with the Captain over there."

"Who doesn't he have a beef with?" Garrett muttered.

Necker shot the younger cop a glance. "Don't let Elmo hear you say that Ted."

"Yeah; maybe I just need some lunch."

"Good idea; make yourself scarce for awhile."

"Thanks Elliot."

Garrett sat down at a diner down the street to think things over. At first he thought the Domino Lady was using Ellen Patrick to scout out her victims. When his coffee arrived though, he knew without a doubt that Ellen Patrick was the masked thief herself.

Pulling out a flask, he poured a healthy amount of whisky into the steaming cup and then stirred it with a finger. Realizing what he'd done, the detective looked around for other cops. Seeing none, he sighed. *Last thing I need now is some blue nose trying to turn me over to Wahl or Kynette.*

Cursing mentally, he realized that her costume was right in front of him. *I saw that white dress hanging in her closet next to a black cloak. Didn't even think to look for pockets in it. I could have brought her in already with that mask tied around her pretty, little face.*

Although Davis had allowed Kynette to call in Garrett from the wilderness, the young detective still wasn't in everyone's good graces. Wahl in particular didn't want him brought back in so quickly and told Kynette that with Garrett standing there. The failure to remove Harry Raymond was just confirmation to Wahl that he was right.

"I gotta bring her in and rub Wahl's nose in it," he murmured to himself. "All I need is a way to figure out where she's going to show up next."

Another cup of Irish coffee later and the detective had it figured. Since the masked woman embarrassed the same crooks and politicians that they took payoffs from, the police usually sat back and had a good laugh when the Domino Lady stole from them and left these supposed hard men twisting in the wind. They also didn't pursue any stolen property too hard but figuring out where she went to fence jewelry like that pearl and jade piece would be pretty simple though.

Jade was handled mostly out of Chinatown, but add in those pearls and the number of shops had to go way down. Maybe even just to one or two in Japan town. I need to get back into her house and see if she still has it. If not, then I'll get the names of the fences who could move it. Harry Prescott's in the precinct that watches Japan town and he still owes me a favor.

Garrett got up pleased with his plan. He was so pleased; for once he actually paid for his coffee.

Using the information the Domino Lady gathered from Twisty and a friendly fence in Lakewood, Ellen was able to secure a meeting for her alter-ego with Stony. The empty apartment they would use was near the fence's second hand clothing store he maintained as a legitimate business-man and she knew the area well.

Abandoning the Roadster for tonight, Ellen grabbed the keys to the car used by the gardener and the housekeeper and quickly made her way out onto the streets. Despite the risks, Ellen felt a growing thrill. This would be the Domino Lady's second appearance of the New Year and she looked forward to the adventure. She patted the case on the seat next to her like an old friend.

Already wearing her evening gown, the mask was in the pocket of the cloak on the seat next to her to be slipped on near the meeting. Covering her dimpled shoulders and décolletage was a Nehru jacket from several seasons ago. Atop her luxurious blonde locks was a cloth cap that had fallen out of fashion this spring. Both items of clothing and the auto would draw little attention; especially so close to the second hand store.

Stony walked into the apartment exactly on time. A career criminal with very little time behind bars; he prided himself on being smarter than tough. When he needed to handle a hard time, he had a platoon of men for that. Two of them were waiting in the lobby if this proved to be one of those times.

"Hi Stony. I'm sorry we haven't spoken before, but I suppose you just haven't been in my line of sight yet."

"I know who you are sister and I bet you can't even hit anything with that peashooter." BLAM! The light bulb hanging by his head exploded. There was only one light left in the room.

"Still want me to take that bet Stony?" She gestured with the pistol. "Sit down over there killer. I have a few questions."

"I need to tell my guys to not come in throwing lead first."

The Domino Lady gestured with the .22 to go ahead. He walked back to the doorway.

"Can you hear me?"

"We're coming Boss!"

"Nix that! Get back in the lobby." Stony turned back to address the blonde markswoman.

"Nice shot, but if the cops can't make me talk after one of their weekend vacations, what makes you think you can?"

"Because I really will shoot you in the kneecaps and leave you for the rats and roaches. Also because I took pictures of everything in the folders Twisty had on top of his money box. I put the word out about your lousy security and the rocks will be breaking you into smaller pieces instead of the other way around." That last threat got Stony to sit down.

"OK Domino; you got my attention. You wanna threaten me with the Vice Squad, fine. Just keep in mind that my partners in blue have got a reputation for blowing up the messenger as well; don't push your luck too far."

"I'll take that under advisement, killer."

Proctor looked at her for a moment. "Your reputation is about being a thief. Pretty good one too. I understand hitting Twisty for the cash but what do you want with me?"

"It's funny you mention getting blown up. There's a Spy Squad cop named Tom Garrett just came back to town. He owes me a rather substantial amount of money from before he got sent off to San Francisco. Since I'm certain he doesn't have the cash anymore, I want something of greater value. Since it was Kynette that sent him away, I want something that will make them both feel like they lost a hand."

"I'll take that under advisement, killer."

"Why would I give up a guy who's supposed to protect me and my business?"

"Because you know Garrett doesn't do that. He and a handful of other cops stiff you on bets, booze and broads and there's nothing you can do about it. I think that list includes your former brother-in-law, Stanley."

"You got a good handle on the situation Blondie."

"Well gee Stony; thanks."

"I didn't think you'd ignore all those files. It's worth a lot more than the cash and like I said, you got a good rep. Twisty ain't too smart, but he's as loyal as a bloodhound. He called me soon as he woke up from your little needle trick. His neck still hurts too."

"His neck is in better shape than the people he works over for you."

Stony leaned back in the chair and smiled. "I gotta admit that watching guys like Garrett and that rat Stanley get jerked around is real appealing. What if I help you and you still can't get anything out of him?"

"Then I'll take his badge and make sure his reputation is so damaged not even his boss Kynette will cover for him. Maybe even do the same to Kynette for sending him out of town in the first place."

"You won't get rid of 'em?"

"The cops think I'm an annoyance right now. I shoot one of their own, no matter how rotten he is; I'll never get to steal another pretty in this town again without a dragnet getting thrown over me."

Stony stared at the Domino Lady for a moment. Then he smiled and nodded.

"OK, you've got a deal."

"A deal?"

"Yeah, I tell you where to get the dirt on Garrett and Kynette and you leave my operations alone for the next six months."

The Domino Lady had to admire the man's gall. "Two months." she said with a grin.

"Four."

"Ten weeks."

Stony got up slowly. "You've got a deal. Kynette has an apartment that he uses as an office for the Spy Squad's dirtiest tricks. It's over on 248 Monument, Apartment 310."

"As long as this plays out, you won't see me again until April." She motioned to the closet with her chin.

"Got to wave off the two boys outside first." He walked over to the window and signaled. One of the men outside waved at the thugs in the lobby and they all got in the waiting auto.

"Four tough guys just to handle little old me?"

"I get the feeling now I didn't bring enough." Stony walked into the closet whistling.

The Domino Lady locked it behind him and shoved a chair under the knob. It wouldn't hold the thug for more than a minute, but it would allow her to leave without worrying about being followed. It was time to tell Roge the good news.

The day after the CIVIC meeting, Catherine Edwards had just finished lunch with another society wife. The woman hated her, but loved thinking she and her husband were in the Edwards' inner circle of friends. Occupied with the next item on her to-do list, she never noticed the Packard pull up next to her.

"Good afternoon Catherine. Would you join me in the car please?"

She jumped at the voice and looked around quickly; there were people all around her and she could refuse to get in, but that would only delay whatever he wanted.

"Of course Douglas. So happy to see you again."

She climbed into the backseat next to the smiling man and then the Town Car pulled swiftly away from the curb.

That evening, the Domino Lady was finally able to fence the jewelry from the New Year's Eve heists in Japan town. Jesse Korematsu was the premiere criminal to go to with "hot" pearls. When he was given the description of the necklace stolen, he knew exactly who would purchase it, but it took him almost three weeks to arrange the transaction. It was a one-time best offer and he insisted it had to be done that night.

She would have preferred to accompany Roge, but he could certainly handle getting into Kynette's apartment by himself. Unknown to her, the Japan town precinct informers had been told to look for a "high society looking blonde" entering Korematsu's business. When one of them saw her go inside, he ran quickly to the nearest phone booth.

Ted Garrett was still angry after he didn't find the necklace on his second visit to Ellen's home. He now walked into Korematsu's Curio Shop with his badge out and his right hand on his service weapon, hoping his target would resist arrest a little. The other customers quietly exited as he approached the cloaked woman at the counter. He could see her in the mirror on the front of the cash register. His prey recognized him from Roger McKane's description.

"Those are very large sunglasses Miss. Big enough to cover a mask. Take them off and let's see."

The pretty blonde turned around and slid the sunglasses down to reveal the mask of the Domino Lady. She turned her smile up to blinding, moved close to Garrett ... and buried her left heel in his right instep. Before he could yell, the bombshell vigilante struck him in the throat and used a *Te-Waza* to grab his right arm and throw him into a display of Kimonos and Hanten jackets.

"Catch me if you can Garrett!" With that, she snatched an envelope off the counter and ran out the front door, hoping not to find another police officer. Garrett didn't have another detective with him but there was an off-duty police officer nearby; Sean Coughlin.

Despite the danger, the Domino Lady knew this area well and couldn't help thinking, *I wish I could put $20 on myself to get away!* The problem for her was not hitting the detective chasing her; she was a crack shot. As she told Stony, until now she hadn't injured a policeman, not even a crooked one. The moment she did, the entire police force would come down on her and Owen Patrick would never be fully avenged.

Fortunately, her previous visits to Japan Town (legal and otherwise) had given her a solid knowledge of the back alleys most occidentals wouldn't dream about. She knew that losing Garrett would not be a problem. What happened after that would be the problem. His appearance confirmed that he found the stolen jewelry and had made the link between the Domino Lady and Ellen Patrick.

How do I stop him and keep up the fight?

Ducking around one more corner, she leaned into her run and struck a door leading into a warehouse hard. It barely moved. She forced her arm between the frame and the door and pushed it open another two inches.

That flat-chested shop girl is laughing somewhere.

She wedged her shoulder in again just as she heard running in her direction and a familiar voice. After firing a shot into the bricks near Garrett's head to make him duck across the alley entrance, she began pushing again.

Coughlin saw the masked woman run out of the curio shop and then a few seconds later, a man chasing her, yelling "Stop! Police!" Sean didn't recognize him but he still turned to the young woman he was walking with.

"Kayoko, I have to go and assist the other police officer. If I can, I'll meet you at the restaurant later."

"Be safe." Despite wanting to kiss her, he knew not to embarrass her publicly and instead, simply squeezed her hand. He quickly ran after the slightly limping detective. A few moments later, he caught up to the other man just a shot made him duck behind the opposite corner of the alley entrance.

The young man pulled out his badge and his off-duty pistol. "Police! I'm Patrolman Sean Coughlin; identify yourself!"

Garrett lifted up his own badge. "Detective Sergeant Tom Garrett. I recognize your name Coughlin. Got it from Elmo Wahl."

"What's going on here Sergeant?" Coughlin blinked; he could smell the alcohol on Garrett's breath.

"That's the Domino Lady we've got pinned down."

Ellen looked at the door into the warehouse slowly open. *Not for long Detective!*

"Why isn't Robbery here Detective Garrett?"

"We found her off a wiretap on the fence's phone. The arrest belongs to the Intelligence Division."

Jesse Korematsu's too smart to get caught like that. "He's lying, Coughlin!"

Garrett put his revolver around the corner and sent a bullet her direction.

"Either start shooting or walk away from this now Coughlin and I'll explain it all to you tomorrow morning."

"I'll help out Wahl and the rest of you whenever I can, but there's no way I'm letting you gun down some girl in an alley. We bring her in on her own feet."

The Domino Lady shook her head and muttered to herself. "Heaven help me from shining knights when I already have an escape route." She stopped trying to squeeze through the door and pointed her .22 back down the alley.

"Hang on Miss! I'll get you out of here!"

Garrett finally had a bellyful. "Die with her then Boy Scout!"

He stepped forward and fired his .38 at Coughlin, striking him once in the left arm but before he could pull the trigger a second time, rounds from the Domino Lady's .22 and the younger cop's snub nose buried themselves in Garrett's chest and neck.

Coughlin turned to face the blonde avenger. His left arm hung useless, his hand was not as steady as he wished and his vision was already beginning to blur.

"Detective Garrett didn't have the right to try and gun you down, but I still have to take you in."

The Domino Lady smiled at him. "You can barely raise that .38 officer. Can you stay conscious long enough to arrest me?"

Coughlin returned the grin. "Yes, I believe I can."

"Well, I suppose I should make it easy on you then." The masked bombshell leaned down and put her .22 on the ground. Then, she walked toward him, making sure she bounced just enough with each step to keep the young policeman's eyes on her chest.

As she approached, Coughlin holstered his sidearm and then reached back on his belt for handcuffs. Too late, he realized that he couldn't see her left hand. He quickly brought his right hand forward again, but the Domino Lady grabbed it with her own in a *Kansetsu-Waza* to bring him forward and down. Instead of forcing him hard to the ground and injuring him further however, she put him down carefully before using the syringe.

The last things Coughlin remembered were a pair of soft lips on his own and the words, "Thanks for everything tough guy."

"Who are you?"

McKane reached across the desk and pulled the manager over his desk by his neck.

"Kynette sent me to get something up out of 310."

"Hey! Hey! No need to get rough; just say who you are. You need the key or you got your own?"

"I'll take yours. The call got me at home."

"Sure thing! No problem!" He handed Roger a key ring for 310. As soon as McKane got to the third landing, he made a call.

"Wahl speaking."

"This is Freddie from the apartment. Some guy just came here and roughed me up for the key."

Wahl didn't to ask which apartment, Freddie was told to never call unless someone broke in or was about to.

"Who was it?"

"I didn't ask after he nearly pulled my head off. He's a little taller than me with slicked back, dark hair. Kind of a pretty boy."

Garrett! "I'm coming over now. If he comes down the stairs before I get there, keep him talking."

"You ain't paying me enough to grab him." Freddie whined.

"I ain't paying you for what I know you ain't got weasel. If he leaves, get the license number." Wahl slammed down the phone.

"Necker! Grab the nearest guy I trust and follow me!"

I've hit the mother load. McKane thought. The front room and kitchenette looked like any apartment, but the two bedrooms were set up like evidence rooms.

"OK Roger, don't get lost in all this. The Spy Squad keeps files on everyone. Just grab whatever they have on Mayor Shaw and their own people and get out." It took him a few minutes to find the right files and start throwing them in an empty box. *Move faster, that rat-faced manager had to have called someone.*

Minutes later, Roger grabbed the box and ran out the door; straight into Wahl's left hook. He dropped it into the hallway and stumbled back into the apartment with the detective following. McKane ducked the next punch and put one of his own right onto Wahl's chin; snapping his head back and breaking several of his teeth. The big cop bounced back into the doorframe and McKane slammed his shoulder into Wahl's gut.

Roger slipped past him, but the detective got another left into his kidney as he went by. A second blow got him in the temple and sent him to his knees as Wahl bent over, wheezing.

"What's wrong snooper? Can't handle anything except a cheating wife?"

"Big talk from a guy blowing air like a flounder in a boat." Roger then spun on his knee and hammered his left fist into the side of Wahl's own.

The big Lieutenant howled and hopped backwards; too slow. McKane leaped straight up, crashing the top of his head into Wahl's chin. Elmo spun around and fell head first onto the stairs leading to the fourth floor. Despite splitting a gash over his an eyebrow, Wahl was able to turn over just in time to see Roger kick him square in the groin.

As the big cop bent forward to protect himself, McKane grabbed him by an ear and punched him in the face until Wahl stopped struggling. Roger saw that he was unconscious and let go of his head to fall back on the steps. The younger man sat down on the bottom step and began checking for loose teeth.

"Wahl already went up! Get moving and see why he didn't signal out the window!"

McKane looked down the stairwell to see the other two cops start up the stairs. He sighed, stripped off Wahl's tie and wrapped it around his hand. Then he pulled Wahl's cuffs off his belt and slipped them over the tie.

As he got up, Roger noticed the sap that fell out of Wahl's pants and picked it up. Then he backed up four steps from the landing and crouched low, listening for when they made that last turn up the stairs.

OK; let's see how many more times I can get punched in the head tonight before I pass out.

Once she made certain no one had followed her back to the sedan, the mask and cloak were shed once again for the Nehru jacket and cloth cap. Ellen drove home both excited and concerned. Coughlin was more concerned about doing the right thing than catching her. Would that and her helping him stop Garrett keep the motorcycle cop from relating her part in the Spy Squad detective's death?

The envelope of cash from the jewelry was no comfort as she parked the sedan and walked up to the house.

Roge is back. Good, maybe this night isn't a total loss then.

Ellen walked into the study to find McKane bleeding on her leather sofa, one eye swollen shut and the other almost matching. He was also drinking her scotch from the bottle with his feet up on a cardboard box.

"Hi Ellen. Did you and the Domino have as good a night as I did? I sure hope not."

The next evening, the CIVIC leader is startled by a voice in his home office.

"Good evening Mr. Clinton."

"Who are you? I'm not afraid of anyone in a mask I'll have you know." He nodded at her hand. "Or that little automatic you have there."

"That's good to hear Clifford. Then you might be able to use this." She tossed copies of the records Kynette had kept on Wahl and other police officers. There were even files that implicated Chief Davis and cast a large shadow over Mayor Shaw.

"I don't think it's enough to bring down the Mayor, but perhaps it will cripple his operations enough to ..."

"... give us a fighting chance?" Clinton looked at the masked woman with distaste. "You'll forgive me if I don't take your word in all this."

The Domino Lady shook her head. "I don't expect you to; what I do expect is for you to check these documents against the box of Spy Squad files the District Attorney received in his office this afternoon." She dropped her hand under the cloak and secured the .22 in the garter. Then she brought both hands out so the restaurateur could see them.

"I think you'll both be pleased. Good night." With that, she drew her hood over her face and left through the French door she had picked her way into earlier. By the time Clinton walked over and looked out, she was gone.

When he opened the file, the first item he noticed was the calling card clipped to the top of the contents.

"Compliments of the Domino Lady"

"You nearly scared me to death yesterday, showing up like that Douglas."

"I just wanted to make sure you had convinced Miss Patrick with your story Catherine."

"It was fairly easy. She wants to believe that she can somehow find and punish her Father's killers. I just gave her a believable target."

"It's that common background which concerns me Catherine. All this," He waved his hand at their surroundings, "can rapidly disappear if you appear to grow soft on her."

"Ellen is on her own. When my Father died, I was left with a pen full of cows and a desk drawer full of debts. I had to sell everything just to break even so I could get off that farm and start over. She gets no sympathy from me."

"That's good to know. I mention it because you also seem to be growing genuinely fond of Anson."

"I suppose I am; he does treat me very well. That said, I fully remember that he's an assignment first. No more dairy farms for me."

"What if I tell you he's no longer necessary?"

"Anson has already lived a long, better life than most people dream of. His two sons have no interest in the family business and more than enough assets are already noted in his will to be liquidated for them. They are fully aware of this and I have no doubt they've already begun to spend their inheritance. In another year, one of them may even make that decision for you."

Catherine picked up her drink and looked at the interplay between the Scotch and the ice cubes. "I'll move out of here with only the funds stipulated plus the furniture and any personal items he purchased for me. Along with full control over the properties that are considered valuable to you and your associates of course."

"I thought Anson was leaving you the family house in his will?"

"He is, but the boys aren't happy about it. There's a weekend house in Malibu that will suit me fine. Anson is making the change next month."

Douglas smiled. "I've been there. As fast as Los Angeles is growing, the land alone under that house will be worth more in a few years than this place and everything in it."

"Yes, Anson knows that and feels it would be an appropriate final joke on his ungrateful offspring. Here he comes now."

"Douglas! So glad you could join us for dinner."

The two men shook hands. "I never miss the opportunity Anson. Ginny sends her love but she had to go see her Mother in Monterey. I put her on the 4 o'clock train before I came here."

"That's fine Douglas. She can join us next time." He gestured toward the dining room. "Shall we?"

"That bruise on your face is fading already."

Ellen gave McKane a wry look. "In another day or two, with the right makeup, no one will notice. It's going to take another week or two in your case Mister McKane."

Roger wisely changed the subject. "According to the papers, the police are looking for an unidentified blonde suspect. A male, blonde suspect."

Ellen shrugged, "Domino was certain Coughlin would cover for her."

"Maybe he just doesn't want to admit that she pulled one over on him."

"I believe her words were, 'The male ego covering for itself is just as reliable as a bullet.' Sounds accurate to me Roge."

McKane winced. "She doesn't have a very good opinion of men does she?"

"It's OK dear," Ellen leaned over and patted her companion's hand, "that's what she has me for." Pulling back, she asked, "How is Harry doing?"

"Recovering nicely and much happier when I told him what was about to happen. He agreed with me though that it's not enough to bring down Shaw or Davis. I'm sorry Ellen."

Ellen ran a finger around her mimosa glass and looked at her brunch companion.

"It's OK Roge. With what we did find, Kynette and his Spy Squad will certainly go to trial. It'll be impossible for them to pin all of this on Garrett. When it comes down to it, there's nothing beyond Catherine's guess that Shaw or Davis were involved with my Father's death. As you said, Shaw tries to avoid killing. I'll accept what we can get."

McKane sat for a moment and looked at the woman he respected more than most men and still cared for. "We finally get a chance at brunch and you're so serious Ellen. Did those lovely legs of yours get such a close shave that you're thinking clearly now?"

Roger's words shook her out of her mood.

"I'm just recalling what a friend of mine said last year. Knowing when to step off the parade field and so forth."

"Parade field?" Roger frowned. "Sounds like a man in uniform has your attention Ellen."

Brown eyes flashed with amusement as she wagged her finger at McKane. "Don't be jealous Roge; he's old enough to be my father. He's also in Panama."

The tall detective grinned ruefully. "I'm always jealous where you're concerned Ellen dear."

"I guess that's not so bad when it comes down to it. There's no need to worry though, I'm not going anywhere for a long time." She lifted her glass toward McKane. "Shall we toast to accepting, but not settling for, what we achieved this week?"

"Hear, hear!"

Ellen finished the drink, put her glass down and looked Roger McKane directly in the eyes. "Now about that to-do-list."

The End

KEVIN FINDLEY—was raised by a kindly couple in a small town in Kansas. Unfortunately, he misplaced his blue suit and red cape as a child, so he has been a freelance writer for the last two years. For three years before that, he edited websites for a number of commercial businesses.

Prior to that, he served 20 years in the U.S. Air Force. He retired as a Logistics Specialist with the rank of Major back in 2009. During that time, he was able to travel and live in various places to include Austria, Japan, Egypt and many more. Surprisingly, he is still allowed in all of those countries. He is married with two kids still at home and more scattered throughout the U.S.

His wife is very happy he finally listened to her and took up writing as something other than a hobby. It keeps him home, makes a few bucks and keeps him out of trouble for the most part. If you want to tell him how much you loved his second tale of the Domino Lady or even if you didn't you can contact him at www.linkedin.com/pub/kevin-findley/35/208/36a/. Expect more from him at Airship 27 and other Pulp-related corners of the internet.

More adventures of Domino Lady!

PULPDOM'S SEXIEST AVENGER!

The Domino Lady first appeared in the pulps in 1936. After graduating from the Berkeley College in California, Ellen Patrick goes off to Europe on a joy filled jaunt. Her trip is cut short when her widowed father, D.A. Owen Patrick, is murdered by gangsters. Upon her return home she learns the corrupt authorities have no intention of finding her father's killers. Thus she puts on a domino mask and a backless white dress to avenge him. Though arming herself with a small .22 automatic and a syringe full of knockout serum, the Domino Lady's most effective weapon was her sensual beauty, which often distracted her opponents until she could turn the tables on them.

Now new pulp writers, Greg Hatcher, Gene Moyers, Tim Bruckner and Kevin Findley offer up four brand new adventures of Los Angeles' most notorious, and sexiest, crime-fighter of them all, the Domino Lady!

PULP FICTION FOR A NEW GENERATION!

AIRSHIP27HANGAR.COM FOR AVAILABILITY

www.ingramcontent.com/pod-product-compliance
Lightning Source LLC
Chambersburg PA
CBHW051131260626
47170CB00005B/1765